Notes From the Crawl Room

Notes From the Crawl Room

A Collection of Philosophical Horrors

A.M. Moskovitz

BLOOMSBURY ACADEMIC
LONDON • NEW YORK • OXFORD • NEW DELHI • SYDNEY

BLOOMSBURY ACADEMIC
Bloomsbury Publishing Plc
50 Bedford Square, London, WC1B 3DP, UK
1385 Broadway, New York, NY 10018, USA
29 Earlsfort Terrace, Dublin 2, Ireland

BLOOMSBURY, BLOOMSBURY ACADEMIC and the Diana logo are
trademarks of Bloomsbury Publishing Plc

First published in Great Britain 2022

Series design by Adriana Brioso
Cover image: Jebel Ali port, Dubai, UAE.
(© NASSER YOUNES/AFP/Getty Images)

A catalogue record for this book is available from the British Library.

A catalog record for this book is available from the Library of Congress.

ISBN: HB: 978-1-3501-9187-7
       PB: 978-1-3501-9188-4
       ePDF: 978-1-3501-9189-1
       eBook: 978-1-3501-9190-7

Typeset by RefineCatch Limited, Bungay, Suffolk
Printed and bound in Great Britain

To find out more about our authors and books visit www.bloomsbury.com
and sign up for our newsletters.

Contents

In 2018, these seventeen short stories were found in a desk drawer in the former office of Dr A.M. Moskovitz. They are collected here for the first time. All characters and events in this publication, other than those clearly in the public domain, are fictitious and any resemblance to real persons, living or dead, is purely coincidental. Nevertheless, the following pages contain references to violences, both institutional and interpersonal, so readers are advised to continue with caution.

Introductory Essay: Uroborotic Horror

By Susan K. Lang

I must admit to being slightly surprised when I was first asked to write an introduction for this compendium, since Moskovitz's academic background in analytic metaphysics lies several leagues from my own, in psychoanalysis. I knew something of his story, but few of the details. Nonetheless, I agreed to look at the submitted manuscript. I sat at my kitchen table and leafed through the pages – and the more I read, the more I found myself turning away. I was repulsed by the content of the stories, their form and – yes – by what little I knew of their genesis. There was something interesting in this repulsion, however; it came from somewhere obscure within me.

Readers may be tempted to find in these peculiar texts some foreshadowing of the incidents for which the author later became known. For present purposes, it will be helpful to bracket off the reports of the fires, the collapses, the disappearances (which were anyway well-documented, online and off). Better, I think, to try and understand the conditions that produced these writings as they were written (an activity we can engage in without fear of legal reprisals). This project leads me back, as all my research eventually does, to the concept of the uroboros and what I have called the "uroborotic subject".

The uroboros or ouroboros is an ancient Egyptian symbol depicting a serpent engaged in the act of self-consumption, the consumption of its own tail. The earliest instances of this motif appear in the *Enigmatic Book of the Netherworld* found in the desecrated tomb of Tutankhamun, and date from the fourteenth century BCE. This millennia-old token is taken to symbolise variously: eternal cyclic renewal, the circle of life, and the transmigration of souls. For the Jungians it is the basic mandala of alchemy or, sometimes, a representation of the pre-ego "dawn state", depicting the undifferentiated experience of the infant. In my own work, I have found it productive in relation to psychoses of self-reference. The uroborotic subject is horrified by their own subjectivity, their agency and – at a more schematic level – by circular reasoning, the infinite and the paradoxical. The stories collected in this compendium are all, in their different ways, encircled by this logic.

Uroborotic horrors sometimes manifest in anxieties around architecture. Reading Moskovitz's work, I was reminded of the case of one "Michael P.", who alongside other neuroses exhibited a peculiar form of nominal inversion. During our sessions together, I found he frequently confused the architectural and the organic; he would refer to walls as "skin" and eyes as "windows". He complained that he could not "find a way out", except sometimes by way of a set of "stairs" which led, alternately, "nowhere" or "all the way down".

In classic psychoanalytic theory, the building often stands as a cipher for the subject's body. Basements are the bowels, where the unconscious trauma sits and frets. The attic is the head, the space of reasons – a place of special horror for anyone trained in analytic philosophy. As the author comments, the ivory tower is "carved from bone and body-parts". The boiler-room, meanwhile, is the heart, where the "canker sits"; it is the centre of the circulatory system which pumps poisoned blood and other toxins around the body via a network of corridors, stairs and chimney flues. This conceptual intertwining of organic and architectural bodies, which I saw with Michael P., is made explicit in this collection (e.g. "The Gravesend Institute"). There is no obvious anus here – and that, again, is a distinctive feature of uroborotic symbology.

Like Michael P., Moskovitz's characters find themselves trapped within architectural bodies. They fear embodiment. They are horrified by their physicality and take great pains to disassociate from it. In doing so they simultaneously reassert their bodily presence. This is the dualist's nightmare. They are running from their ability to run (the horror is compounded). They are the corridor down which they are themselves pursued.

Uroborotic logic also explains the author's neurotic engagement with language. In 2006, I treated a graduate student, "Rebecca S.", who came to me to discuss her "writer's block". The block in question was of an unusual kind; she would only ever write in negations. She would compose, often in quite beautiful, elegiac prose, the precise opposite of what she actually believed. Likewise, the characters here (and the author himself) seem drawn to un-write what they have written. These texts turn in on themselves, revile themselves, and possess interminable contradictions. The author attempts to distance himself from these cycles through processes of ventriloquism and the use of pseudonyms (Benedict March, Cousin Vincent and Susan K. Lang).

Sitting at my kitchen table, I remembered the conversations with my partner about the various apocrypha circulating around these texts. Moskovitz was said to have written them in a dream state or under the influence of psychoactive drugs. I recall several users of Twitter supposing him to have been a conglomerate of Russian "bots", while others thought he was nothing more than the output of a random text generator. The few philosophers who acknowledged his existence described Moskovitz as an egoist and a fantasist. "Self-indulgent and self-obsessed" said one. Self-indulgence is not unexpected; the snake that eats its own tail sees itself as the centre of the universe. This solipsism connects to the excessive and onanistic writing style. Even a cursory glance through the collected stories reveals a baroque styling. This logophilia or logorrhea – the repeated and desperate repetition of unnecessarily polysyllabic terms – is indicative both of an oral *and* an anal fixation; the uroborotic subject is constantly playing with their words (or verbal excreta) and themselves. They are also constantly reiterating their reiterations and these texts are ordered by logo-rhythmic repetitions. Not only does the author return to the same themes (moons, smiles, hands, bone china), but the same ugly phrases regularly recur like the subjects of a fugue: "There was probably nothing to worry about", "It was probably fine." The author is swallowing and regurgitating his disavowals at the same time as swallowing and regurgitating himself.

The nurturing oral mother is the second of Sacher-Masoch's three women. I have always been fascinated by the conceptual connections between masochism and uroborotic horror. The masochist says paradoxically: "I assert my denial", "I ask to be dominated", "I relinquish my power". The uroborotic subject issues these same statements out of horror at their own agency, but doing so necessarily re-inscribes that agency. At its root, this horror is a determinately social condition legislated by privilege, which is why another patient, "Samuel K." – who "relinquished" his inheritance to live a life of "asceticism" – is another example of an uroborotic subject. Privilege, whether racialised or class-based, cannot be relinquished. Horrified by their own agency, these individuals are obsessed by it too. The uroboros is a symbol of insatiable individualism and (in psychoanalytic theory) auto-fellatio.

Moskovitz was trained in analytic philosophy, specialising in metaphysics – and while not inevitable, his uroborotic tendencies are far from surprising. Analytic philosophy creates a fetish both of the individual thinker and of rational argumentation – and nothing is so corrosive to the analytic mind as the *paradox*, which is another item of horror here. This sentence is a lie. To consider the paradox is to be trapped. To cross the boundary between truth and falsity is to be abject. Like those childhood nightmares in which we are chased in endless circles, the paradox takes us round and round the garden, a circus-ride of circular reasoning. If the sentence is true then the sentence is false, so the sentence is true, so the sentence is false (...).

Formally speaking, paradoxes revolve around three elements: contradiction, self-reference and circularity. For example: "What happened to Moskovitz was possible and impossible". This statement, made in witness testimonies, contradicts itself. Likewise: "The author could not have done what he did in fact do." I remember reading the witness statements in which witnesses described themselves as "non-credible", and issued self-undermining phrases such as "I am not to be trusted". In reports of the incidents, bystanders identified with the author and doing so produced a vicious circularity. They did not see what they saw. We find another articulation of the paradoxical in the note found by the caretaker, Daniel P., tacked to the top of the papers retrieved from the author's desk. There, Moskovitz wrote in smudged and shaking letters: "These are my words. Read them, but whatever happens, do not read them." A warning and an entreaty that I echo as an introduction to this collection.

The circular snake creates a hole, a vacuum, an absence, which manifests in the last and most distinctive feature of uroborosis, which in the past I have called the "Empty Man". This horrible figure, the product of the uroborotic imagination, appears in many of my patients' case-notes. He is described as wearing a hood or head-covering, as being faceless or open-mouthed or simply "blank". He figures – sometimes explicitly – in this collection, though the author does not like to linger on him. It is easy to understand why. The Empty Man, the manifestation of the subject's own self-denial and self-negation, cannot comfortably be subjected to scrutiny. He is the light from which one shrinks. His emptiness is unbounded; it leaks. Indeed, there is something about the references to the "empty man" reminiscent of reports of mass hysteria in the nineteenth century (e.g. "Spring-heeled Jack" and "the Mad Gasser of Mattoon"). That there is a contagious element to this condition is also suggested by the relations between my patients – and by the disconcerting feeling I experienced on reading the manuscript. Sitting at my kitchen table, repelled and compelled by these stories, I was struck by the thought that the reports about the author were nothing more than figments, that Moskovitz was himself an "empty man" and that I was suffering from the exact condition I diagnosed in others. It is a thought that continues to trouble me – and draws me, horribly, ineluctably, to read these stories again.

The Ring of Gyges

From a distance it looks like an ordinary ring. A circlet of gold, a wedding band. Perhaps it catches the light, draws the eye. Just a ring, you think, if unblemished, if oddly bright. Closer inspection, however, reveals an almost perfect torus. It is edgeless and presumably bulky to wear, though this does not lessen its appeal. It has neither inside nor outside, its surface is a smooth and unbroken curve that touches the air equally in all places. It is a single plane that has somehow tricked its way into three-dimensional space. As the shepherd Gyges discovered all those years ago, this peculiar geometry confers on its wearer a most singular property.

Her bed was adrift. Around her, shadows ran slippery as the room swam and the chair, cupboard, dresser, nightstand and door shifted, merging into and over one another. She reached for Richard's hand and clutched it. He turned in his sleep, sniffed, nuzzled, murmured, then his mouth grew slack.

There was nothing to worry about.

The feeling would pass.

It was remarkable how little comfort Richard's hand offered. Jess released her grip and stared at his thick fingers, pale and tensing to the rhythm of his dreams. It was an upturned crab, she thought. She rolled over and stared at the mess of shapes that now constituted her bedroom. Lines or her eyes blurred. She needed to calm down. She needed to sleep.

She tried to settle her thoughts into some semblance of order. It had been a pleasant evening. She had drunk too much as always but she was glad she'd gone. She was glad. It had been, as Marcia kept saying, a "wonderful send-off".

"He hasn't *died*," Jess had replied. "He's just retiring."

She could never tell if Marcia was laughing sarcastically.

The catering staff had decided to place the tables on the patio and Jess had just about managed to navigate her chair through the throng to find herself a plateful of carrot sticks. She wondered again why Marcia had insisted on the garden. She half-suspected it was a personal attack and half-suspected she was being paranoid.

It had been a lovely evening, she told herself. The garden had been lovely, the roses too. Even the speeches had been a little bit lovely. And Grover had enjoyed it – and wasn't that the main thing? "You look beautiful Jessica," he'd said to her, "Radiant." He had been sanguine at the prospect of leaving.

"I'm out," he'd said, leaning down to tuck a rose behind her ear. He even listened to Marcia's speech with good grace, and anyone who didn't know them, and didn't catch the tensing of their jaws and the sharpness of their elbows, might easily have mistaken the two old academics for friends.

Yes, it had been a lovely evening, a great success. There were no scenes, very few arguments, and exactly the right amount of revelry. The sun had shone, the wine sparkled. It was, as everyone said, the perfect way to mark the day.

"End of an era."

Jess rolled in bed, readjusting her pillow, and closed her eyes. It made no appreciable difference. Her eyelids contained the same fluid blankness that swam around the bedroom, that had swum around Grover. But there was no reason for her to feel this agitated. It had been a trick of the light and nothing to worry about. She was hot. Too hot. She rolled down the bed-covers and flapped her t-shirt, letting the air flow across her stomach. Beside her, Richard grumbled. It sounded like a grumble at any rate. More likely, he was just snoring. She had a tendency to interpret unexpected noises as criticism. That was part of the problem, she thought. She was too sensitive. Too sensitive and too hot.

It had been a trick of the light, that was all.

She would talk to Richard about it in the morning. Not that there was anything to talk about, but she would talk to him and he would reassure her in that matter-of-fact way of his and they would laugh about her neuroses. He would tell her she needed a holiday – which was true – and that she was anxious about the teaching assessments – which was also true. For a moment, she considered waking him, but he would be grumpy (even if he pretended not to be). His hand had scuttled under his pillow. The pale wet of his eyeballs were visible through a crack in his half-open lids.

Around her, the room seethed.

Richard, lying beside her, had lost his edges.

Everything was open.

It had been nothing – a visual hiccough, that was all, a blip. She wasn't going blind, her retina hadn't detached, she wasn't suffering from migraine with visual auras. She had not had, nor was she in the process of having, a stroke. Despite what the internet search engines had suggested on her taxi-ride home, it had not been the result of "selective attention", or "hemispatial neglect". It had simply been one of those mundane everyday illusions. The face staring at you from a window, which turns out to be your own. Whatever she'd seen, or rather whatever she'd failed to see, was not in any way "sinister".

There was nothing to worry about.

She couldn't breathe. She thought: what was there to inhale or exhale? The room seeped. She fumbled for the glass on her nightstand. Invisible. She struggled to a sitting position. The water, when it met her lips, was unpleasantly warm, but the trembling stopped. The liquid trickled its way through the chambers in her chest. Boundaries began to reassert themselves. She needed to calm down. She needed to–

Perhaps therapy was a good idea after all. Whenever Richard suggested it, she sidestepped the issue. It was a waste of money – she didn't have the time – it would make her more stressed – she didn't deserve it. But maybe he was right – not because she was "seeing things" (which she wasn't), but because it was three o' clock in the morning and she was gripped by the thought that she might have.

It was ridiculous. She had seen *nothing*. But that was precisely the problem. She had been unable to see something, like the woman in the story who grew blind to objects on her left-hand side. That was "hemispatial neglect", which Jessica didn't have. The moment in the garden had lasted for no more than twenty seconds, and from the frantic searches in the taxi she knew that hemispatial neglect lasted for much longer.

The green digits of her alarm clock blinked. Objects dissolved and she was struck by a feeling of flatness, an inability to move herself, as though she were being written from the inside out. She clutched at her chest. She couldn't breathe.

The feeling would pass.

It – the moment in the garden – had been nothing. It had been too short even to be what psychologists referred to as an "episode". Had she fallen asleep she would have forgotten about it. She closed her eyes, or perhaps she didn't, and the room and her thoughts swam. Dark stars shone.

She had been on the patio.

The lawn had been uneven, impassable with her chair, so she sat by the dips as Marcia strolled to the middle of the grass and struck the side of her glass with a knife. Jess could hear it, its brittleness. "Hear ye, hear ye," Marcia called. The faculty and their friends flocked over, leaving Jess to watch from the side-lines. Perhaps Marcia had engineered it that way. Perhaps, but Jess hadn't minded. She sat, working her way through a pile of vegetable batons, while the department head rolled through the obligatory anecdotes. Grover was leaving, but remained part of the fabric of the institution.

"It is a puzzle over which mereologists will long wonder, where Grover ends and the department begins."

Jess remembered: laughter, the raising of glasses, the barks of magpies. From her spot in her chair on the patio, the only visible faces had been Marcia's (taut, satirical), and Grover's (moon-like, beaming). He stood to one side, half-shadowed by a cherry tree, cheeks as red as the fruit that hung overhead – and Jess had felt a surge of affection for her former supervisor, watching him nodding along to the well-worn stories.

These stories were followed by a toast – then a response from Grover – then another toast. Another. The light had dappled. A digression into departmental politics and people began drifting back towards the tables. Humus. Tsatziki. A peculiarly pink mousse that Jess thought might have been meat. Grover leant against the cherry tree and laced his little fingers together, idly rubbing that large gold ring of his. Round and round. Round and round the garden.

Her chest tightened.

He had turned to her. He had smiled at her. An old man, a lecturer, a man of letters, smiling at a former student, his protégé. Nothing was quite so normal. The gold ring glinted. It had been a slip of the eye.

It had just *seemed* as if he'd disappeared.

It had just *seemed* as if he'd bled away into the garden air.

It had been a trick of the light, that was all. The sun's rays glancing from an open window. The dappling of the cherry leaves. Any number of illusions. And yet–

She had blinked – once, twice, three times – but the spot beside the tree remained empty. Not dark, or in any way obscure, but somehow *voided*. She had seen the flaking tree-trunk, the tangle of rhododendrons, but it was as if the man had been bleached from existence. As if–

But she'd made a mistake. It was an optical distortion, caused by the sun or the shadows cast by the department building – and a moment later he had returned as if he had never gone away – so nothing had happened, not really. And no one else had noticed and Marcia had continued her speech, and the crowd had chuckled and cheered. "It's amazing how someone with so little talent has had such a glittering career!" Grover's uninhibited laughter caught in the branches of the cherry tree, unsnagged itself and rose. Nobody but Jess seemed to have experienced this visual irregularity, and had it not been for that *smile*, she thought, she might not have noticed either. But she had. Or she hadn't.

She needed to sleep. Everything would feel much more reasonable in the morning. The house creaked for no other reason than that it was an old house, with old floorboards that warped with the weather. She had already looked through the rooms, one by one, and there had been no one there, except Richard sitting in bed, with a book in his lap, asking her how her evening had gone.

"End of an era," she'd murmured.

She'd already checked to make sure the front door was locked. Twice, in fact. It would be mad to haul herself out of bed again – just as mad, she tried not to think, as imagining a man's vanishing. And she wasn't mad, she was just anxious. Outside, the clouds rolled across the moon. The room lost its edges and she was held by the thought that this was a nowhere place, boundaryless and fluid. Everything around her, the dresser, the nightstand, and Richard, her snuffling, sweaty Richard, drifted, as if surrounded by fog, and for a moment she was gripped by a desperate hope that she was dreaming. She was teetering on that careful edge, between wakefulness and sleep, and all of this was the product of her imagination.

His smile: it had been the smile of a children's magician, the smile of a man with a secret he no longer wished to keep. "Watch this," that smile had said, and she'd watched, but there was nothing up his sleeves, there was nothing under his hat. In fact, there were no sleeves and no hat, and no man at all, just an empty man-shaped space beside a cherry tree. There had been nothing *to* watch. That had been the horror of it.

Emptiness seeped, expanding in the hollows of her body.

The clouds shifted. Roiled. Slivers of moonlight touched her pillow. She kept still, fighting the emptiness creeping, clawing, rising in her throat. She was in the nowhere place, a circle without a rim, a hole without an edge – and outside, the full moon shone, a pale, horrible, white face, watching, round like a golden ring, filled in.

You can easily slide it onto your finger. It doesn't matter which finger, it will always fit. It fits so snugly you are immediately unsure whether or not you are wearing it. But it is undeniable that you are. What a strange thing, to wear an object that has neither inside nor outside. The ring digests being and collapses order. The space of the intimate loses its clarity, just as the space of the exterior loses its void. Invisible, you are a single, unique dimension and you are everywhere and no one is unknown to you, and this, as Gyges came to know, is power.

Cousin Vincent

Dear Cousin,

I apologise in advance for what I fear will be a rather frenetic letter. I write to you in a state of some disarray, for reasons that shall shortly become apparent.

Before I enter the substance, substantia, *ousia*, of my missive, I would ask you to repair, if you could, to some "private chamber" such that no errant eye may read these words. I am not by my nature a nervous man, but present circumstances license a certain degree of caution.

Let me tell you first that while my thesis is complete, I have decided to abjure the *viva voce* and will soon be taking leave from my college. Dear cousin, you may think this untoward given the ten long years I have invested in my doctoral research. I trust that by the end of this letter you will not think it so very strange.

Those preliminaries aside, let us begin.

I do not imagine the news of Professor O'Connor's death, in January this year, has yet reached the outer limits of Basingstoke, but I believe his name will be familiar to you. I hope it shall, in light of the aforementioned decade spent studying his work. To be sure, the ramblings of your aged cousin may never have held your full attention, but if anything has stuck it will be the name of Andrew Marvell

O'Connor – the last great luminary of analytic philosophy – a light, dear cousin, which has this year been sadly extinguished.

As I have told you, on a number of occasions, the focus of my research has been O'Connor's much neglected *early* work. There are entire libraries dedicated to his later tracts – considered his most mature and elegant – but little on the (scant few) essays he produced in his younger years. It is the perennial ambition of the doctoral student to "carve a niche" for himself and my aim in the course of the writing of this dissertation has been to become an expert in O'Connor's "Bachelor Period". I fancy I have succeeded – but at some cost.

There is a reason these essays are much neglected; they are dull, dear cousin, dreadfully dull. It is the source of mild amazement to new initiates that the author of the coruscatingly brilliant *Mind and Power* also penned the lugubrious "Emendation to Professor Figgis's Theory 'D'" (alongside other equally turgid texts).

Nevertheless, following the advice of my illustrious (if elusive) supervisor, these early works formed the furrow I have doggedly ploughed over the last ten years. My labours have not been entirely fruitless. My work on O'Connor's doctoral thesis has found a home in the second most prestigious British journal of the history of analytic metaphysics and I have received no fewer than *three* citations in last year's Proceedings of the Socratic Society.

I am being immodest, but I trust you now have a better sense of the effect of O'Connor's death on your decrepit relative. *Id est*, I was saddened. At the same time, I confess (to you, dear cousin, but no one else) that his "passing" struck me as not an *unmitigated* disaster. You will think me callous, perhaps, but I have written often of the obstacles faced by those with ambitions for the academy, especially (I may add) for those of advanced years. It is a cut-throat business, dear cousin, and any advantage – intellectual, financial, spiritual – is not to be lightly dismissed. It is for these reasons that, through the offices of my supervisor, I set about procuring myself an invitation to the great man's funeral.

The event took place on a blustery afternoon in deep February. It was, as you may expect, a crowded affair. You will remember Aunt Ethel's "do"; you may treble the number of attendees and quadruple the length of the service. The great and the good of London *literati* were all present in their weeds of mourning and I took considerable care to introduce myself to as many as decorum would allow. It was a vigorous reception – and alongside the Proctors of King's and Queen Mary's I managed to position myself at the sherry table next to one Dr Benjamin Sallow.

Dr Sallow had been O'Connor's research assistant – and indeed, the man to have found the body.

I wonder whether you saw the obituaries. They were overwhelmingly biographical in tone, foregrounding the Professor's *bios*, while shying away from the precise details of *thanatos*. They offered vague euphemisms – most likely, at the request of the family – alluding to his "instability of mind" and "depressed spirits". The word "tragedy" has surfaced more than once.

I can assure you it was hardly my intention to interrogate Dr Sallow about the gruesome particulars. As you may have surmised from the preceding, and from knowledge of your cousin's personal concerns, my interests lay elsewhere: in the status of the great man's unpublished papers and the intention of his estate regarding them.

Obtaining this information from Dr Sallow was no mean feat. Benjamin Sallow has always been a furtive creature, but on that day he had a frightened, almost haunted air. I had expected him to be melancholic, certainly, but not so very tremulous. At the time I paid it little mind, but I have known it in my memories since, that his lambent gaze was ever lingering on my *hands* (of which I guarantee, there is really nothing noteworthy). He was, I recall, unnervingly preoccupied with my fingers – and knuckles – and it took me great effort to commandeer his attention. Eventually, I asked after the papers. It became quickly apparent that I was but the latest in a long line of scholars interested in O'Connor's personal effects. I remember the word "vultures" being used by a member of the family – and not nicely either.

Dear cousin, I'm ashamed to say that I displayed a lack of dignity ill-befitting a man of my years and moral intellect. I offered the good doctor *money* (though I am not a man of means). You will be relieved to hear it was refused, with a shake of the head and a slither of the tongue. Yet caught up in a muted hysteria, I persisted: I set to *begging*. In full view of the Professor's remains (what remained of them), I asked Dr Sallow for any small item he might pass my way – scribblings, marked-up proofs, jotted notes. I would have settled for a shopping list – and with every day that passes, dear cousin, I wish that is all he had relinquished.

The moment I mentioned O'Connor's *early* essays, his "Bachelor Period", Sallow's fluid eyes lifted from my fingertips to my face. A look of consternation, then something close to cunning, flitted in his gaze. He asked for my postal address, which he wrote on a jot of paper, then made his excuses and disappeared back into the throng.

That is the last time I saw the man – but I received a package from him two days later.

I have included the contents of said package inside the box that accompanies this missive, along with a bound copy of my dissertation. You have everything the good doctor sent to me save for the letter, which I have *burned*. Within that box, you shall find – as, to my initial delight, I found – a veritable treasure trove of memorabilia that comprises the remaining effects of O'Connor's life before the publication of *Mind and Power*. Along with the lecture notes and university essays, you will see three diaries, spanning the final three years of his doctoral studies. They are filled with a tiny, tidy script and detail, in the main, his daily affairs in college, what he ate for luncheon and dinner, whom he met for tea, and how many spoonfuls of sugar were applied, etcetera.

Let me a venture an aside. Reading these items, you may comment (as others have done) that there is some similarity in style between his writings and my own. I confess it. It is a common complaint of the doctoral student to be captured by the spirit of the authors they study – though their own writings are typically shadows of their subjects' – but things have markedly worsened of late. "Markedly worsened of late." I wish my pen would issue clearer statements, but the nib and fingers that carry it seem sometimes to have a mind of their own.

In any case – after a couple of hours perusing these objects, my initial excitement became somewhat blunted. While these effects gave unprecedented access to the young O'Connor's private life, his private life was, in truth, as dull as the proverbial ditch-water. The only episodes of interest concerned a romantic dalliance, undocumented in his official Biography, occurring toward the end of the third diary. In September of that year, the young O'Connor met a woman, to whom, he writes, "he was quickly bound, overlapping like a palimpsest", whose mind melted into his own "like molten wax" (an artless reference to Renatus Cartesius). In a December entry, he writes of a "profound coupling" taking place – of "intertwining fingers" and "meeting minds". The year ends before he descends into anything more Rabelaisian.

Erotica aside, I can confidently say that neither his diaries nor his doctoral essays contained even the dimmest glimmerings of the genius found in his later work. You can see for yourself; these papers are simultaneously, and paradoxically, airless and long-winded. Uninspired and uninspiring, they reflect at best a mediocre talent and a prating coxcomb. The young O'Connor delighted in verbosity, in adding unnecessary syllables wherever possible, and as far as I can tell, consistently demonstrated a thoroughgoing disregard for the basics of syllogistic reasoning. On the evidence of Dr Sallow's box, I would say the young Andrew O'Connor was a resolutely tedious being, who had knowledge of greatness, but was singularly ill-equipped to achieve it.

Indeed, aside from the "intertwining fingers", the only item of note was written by an alien hand. In the minor marginalia of a literature overview, I discovered some words by a foreign pen – a broader, more gestural lettering – offering a brief but searing critique of Sir Paul Wimsey's Subjective-objectivism. I shan't trouble you with the details, dear cousin, save to say it was bold enough for me to wonder at its provenance. I found other annotations by the same broad hand, all of them surpassing those of the author in ingenuity. It is clear that O'Connor was disturbed by these musings and attempted to reply to them. These attempts are unnotable, save for the fact that he refers to his interlocutor as "Y", and once as "Y.S." – but I found no other mention of this mysterious fellow, and I'm afraid to say that at this point, exhausted by my failures, and by the affair in general, I replaced the papers in the box and allowed myself to sink into *apatheia*.

What followed were several weeks of low spirits. You may remember my letters from that time, if one can call them that. I was subsumed within a depressive malaise. I was grieving – though whether for O'Connor, or my idea of him, or for my languishing studies, I cannot tell you. I was nearing the completion of my thesis, yet fully aware that my writing lacked that vital spark, the *élan vital*, which renders an otherwise dead text living. I had thought O'Connor's papers might yield some *entelechia*, but it seemed it was not to be. Had it not been for the admonitions and encouragement of my supervisor, I would have abandoned the project and taken up residence in the port bottle. Sometimes, dear cousin, I wish I had done so.

It was later, in the autumn months, that I repaired to Senate House, and in the stillness of those heated book stacks I discovered two things – both notable, neither happy. I come to the climax of my account, dear cousin, and would ask you to suspend your disbelief – for a time – and to remember the character and temperament of your ancient relative. I am not a flighty creature. I am not prone to nervous attacks. I have more often been accused of falling too far toward the other end of the emotional spectrum, being "staid" and "solemn", "slow" and "humourless". Please bear this in mind as you read on.

I cannot tell you precisely how many times I have read Chapter 3 of *Mind and Power*, but it must be in the hundreds. It is a canonical moment in the history of analytic philosophy, the pivot around which the rest of the great monograph revolves, and the catapult which launches the reader into O'Connor's revolutionary metaphysical programme. It is a rarity in the tradition in demonstrating both theoretical rigour and polemical verve – and even sitting in the shadow of Dr Sallow's communiqué, I could not suppress my admiration for the author's humour and acuity – so much so that it took me a lengthy moment to notice a striking similarity between the words before me, and those I had read some weeks prior, as marginalia in a literature overview.

Dear cousin, I will not keep you in suspense; the critique of Sir Paul Wimsey, offered by "Y.S." is replicated *verbatim* in footnote 91, page 312 of *Mind and Power*. This passage appears *without attribution*. Moreover, following a perusal of O'Connor's "Acknowledgements" (which runs at an impressive seventeen pages), I finally discovered a match for those irregular initials, Y.S.: "Yuko Saito". A cursory inspection revealed the same name upon the call-sheet of O'Connor's college contemporaries. To cut a long story into pieces, I became quickly convinced that "Saito", was the author of those annotations.

I can all but hear the cogs in your head turning, dear cousin, and I too thought of that most heinous of academic transgressions: *plagiarism* – the act whereby one man steals the immaterial effects of another man's mind. The prospect arose that this "great man", both object and subject of my exegetical ministrations, might be nothing more than a petty intellectual pickpocket. I realised then (as you must realise now) that such news would devastate the British philosophical establishment, perhaps irreparably.

At the same time, it cannot be denied it would make for an excellent conclusion to my thesis.

That same evening I secured myself an after-hours pass from a librarian of loose morals, and put my research training to good use. With the library catalogue as guide and companion, I set to learning all I possibly could about this creature, Saito. In the first few hours, I obtained the following pieces of information:

Firstly, "Yuko" is a woman's name, and duly possessed in this instance by a woman.

Secondly, said woman is author of several articles and reviews, the majority of which I was able to retrieve from the library archives.

Thirdly, all said papers were written and published in Japanese, and therefore beyond the ambit of my understanding.

I was piqued – but not beaten. At this juncture, I was blessed with one of those rare moments of inspiration, which sometimes visit the lonely scholar. There is a book, dear cousin, infamous amongst philosophers, written by one Dr Theodore Barnhoffer, a gossiping fellow, known primarily as a "campus man" and erstwhile tutor at O'Connor's college in Oxford. This book, *A Philosopher's Life*, is a memoir of sorts, and while lurid and poorly written, it contains a considerable amount of information about the academic *milieu* and its social fluctuations. I found the book and checked the index. I was excited to discover the entry "Saito, Y.", referring me to page 437. I have copied out the relevant passage, for your inspection. I apologise, in advance, for Barnhoffer's florid tone:

"... Now it was summer, and the estimable Grover introduced me to a fellow student of his from Philosophy, whom I remember vividly to have been a woman, and a good-looking woman at that. She hailed from foreign shores, and was possessed of long, raven-black hair worn in the austere style of her people, and though she was rather old for my tastes (the wrong side of twenty-five), I would have made a bid had she not already been *affianced* to another of Grover's cohort. The fiancé in question was a young man who would later become a *great* man, but whose name I will suppress for modesty's sake (his own, rather than mine). I met the woman, Yuko, on several more occasions over the subsequent months, in the company of Grover and aforementioned famous fiancé, and formed a favourable opinion of her as one of the few females in college who appeared to have actually earned her place therein. She was not a brilliant mind, but she was bright and competent, in a manner that one does not expect from representatives of that sex. Doubtless, she benefited from her proximity to the great man, or great *boy* as he was then, and from his intellectual attentions. Unfortunately, she was also subject to fits of hysteria, and I remember one particular episode of impropriety, which found her and her luckless lover engaged in what the English call a "tiff" on the sacred sod outside the college wash-house. Bright she may have been, but *stable* Yuko was not. I recall overhearing her accusing *him* (this luminary) of something she called 'intellectual vampirism'. The idea that *he* was stealing thoughts from *her*, was, and remains, ludicrous, and any doubt in this matter has been settled by the works the man has gone on to produce *after* her untimely death...
[Etc.]"

I sat there in the Senate House Library, reading and rereading this passage. There was a crack in the window by my desk and a breeze crept into the room, unsettling the pages of my books. My teeth chattered, and experiencing that uncanny dental mechanism I felt strangely dispossessed of myself. I would not at that moment have been surprised to hear those chattering teeth enunciate words not of my choosing. Suddenly in the top of that very tall, very pale building, I felt execrably alone. I collected my references and my notes, packaged up my belongings, and I descended the library steps as swiftly as my rheumatic knees would allow.

That month – *last* month in fact – I posted facsimiles of Saito's articles to a translator, and against the express wishes of my supervisor, I began to revise my thesis. I received the Saito translations two weeks later, and you will be unsurprised to learn that each and every one of them confirmed my suspicions that much of O'Connor's work was not original to the man's mind. Even in translation, they find purer, more poetic, more lyrical form in Saito's texts. Barnhoffer's comments aside, the woman was undoubtedly a genius. At the same time as receiving these documents, I obtained confirmation of her death. She had "passed" at the age of twenty-three (more than thirty years ago), following an automobile accident in Berlin. This is all to say I am certain that O'Connor's work constitutes an exceptional case of academic thievery.

Would that this were all.

Dear cousin, over the last few weeks I have been haunted by those elusive diary entries, on "palimpsests" and "interlaced fingers", and by the spectre of Benjamin Sallow's covering letter. I burned it, as I say, but I wish now I had not, and have tried daily (sometimes hourly) to contact the doctor for textual corroboration. He refuses to answer my calls and has moved out of his lodgings in Swiss Cottage. I am in no doubt as to why, given the pains it obviously took him to pen the first version.

Benjamin Sallow's letter was a dismal thing, written in the high analytic style with a series of unnecessary addenda. He described the state of the Professor's body, on discovery, and the contents of the flimsy notice he found beside the corpse. At the time of reading, I felt his letter too horrible an artefact to preserve, so I cast it reflexively into a waiting grate where it turned immediately to ash. It is ironical, I suppose, that much of it is now burned irrevocably into my memory (though such memories are, of course, inadmissible as evidence, in either academic or legal contexts).

According to Dr Sallow, his master's final words were written to the college physician, and were almost incomprehensibly disjointed. Part confessional, part condemnation, they spoke of "mental infestations", "conceptual pickpocketing" and "light-fingers". They flowed between his usual tidy script and a broader, more gestural lettering. Sallow informed me that towards the end of his notice, his master's writing became nigh on indecipherable – and with good reason. When Sallow found the body he saw, immediately and to his horror, that all save the man's index finger and thumb on his left hand had been chewed down to the knuckle. Here, unfortunately, I remember Sallow's wording quite distinctly:

> "In his frenzy of self-destruction O'Connor had somehow managed to daub with those stumps, in his own sanguinous ink, the Japanese word *YAMERU*, which means 'stop.'"

He died choking on his own gristle.

I am a rational man, dear cousin, but I have weighed the evidence, explored the relevant documentation, and the conclusion I have reached lies far beyond the realm of reason. None of these are healthy thoughts, and as such I have decided *not* to submit the attached thesis for *viva voce*. I will offer instead a rough hypothesis here, for posterity, in the expectation (and hope) that you will never read it.

Whatever happened between O'Connor and Saito, whatever "sharing of souls" took place, however their fingers were "interwoven", the result appears to have been, indeed, a form of "intellectual vampirism" (as Saito called it). O'Connor's plagiarism was spiritual in character, the effects lasting beyond his victim's early death. He leeched her thoughts and penned them as his own – but the mechanism by which he did so was not as secure as he might have wished. To write another's thoughts is in some way to become possessed by them. It appears that at the end his writing hand grew wilful.

In recent weeks, I have begun to notice a change in my own writing. Perhaps you see it too? It has become more convoluted than usual, laden with parenthetical asides and syllables. As I mentioned, it is a common complaint among doctoral students to emulate the style of their subject; spend sufficient time with an author and you will start to copy the character of their writing, no matter how diluted. But O'Connor was a plagiarist. I think of Locke and his *thinking fingers*. I find my thoughts moving in unusual directions.

I apologise for the blottings and redactions.

When I look at my hand now, it seems alien to me. It is unwilling, and when I command it to write it enacts the letters but not the spirit. At times, these thoughts seem to be simply the fancies of an exhausted mind (and I am truly exhausted). At others, I fear my fingers are moving of their own accord. This thought pursues me, never more so than when I press nib to paper. Sometimes it is as if the thoughts travel up my pen and become sedimented in the sinews of my flesh. Am I writing or being written?

In any case, I think you will understand my misgivings about the submission of my thesis. I submit my work to you, dear cousin, hoping you shall never read it. I submit it along with this most honest account, and trust (if you peruse it) that you will offer your ancient relative, if not credence (please, not credence), then sympathy, for I need it dearly.

I travel now to Scotland, where I will attempt to refresh myself in the Highland air, and consider my future, such as it may be. I will not write again, but perhaps we may contact each other by the 'phone.

I trust you and your family are well.

Ever your cousin,

Vincent

By which we learn that "Snow is White"

Steam rose from the mess of feathers.

Nearby, on a curb, stood a small, well-kept child staring with interest at the bloody smear. The child might have stood there indefinitely, mouth open, eyes wide, had its parent not scooped up a mittened hand and dragged it off in the direction of the high street.

"Come *on*, Orlando. We're late to see Nana."

Samuel checked his watch. Then, turning away from the flattened pigeon, he began walking in the direction of the library. He was getting cold and didn't want Sara to see him shivering. He imagined his teeth chattering, *h-h-h-hello*, his nose unpleasantly wet. He wanted – no, he *needed* – to be impressive, to stride into the foyer, red-cheeked and grinning, rubbing his hands with all the confidence he never actually felt.

It was still a mystery to him where he had found the courage to ask her. It was very un-Samuel to ask a girl on a date. She'd been uncertain at first – but eventually she'd smiled that dimpled smile and said, *Well why not?* Unable to think of a reason, she agreed to meet him at seven o'clock on Thursday, which was today, outside the cinema. Seven o'clock was earlier than he would have liked but the film was a horror film and that was something. He hoped – expected even – that she would feel the need to clutch his hand at least once during the screening. He would squeeze back reassuringly. He hoped his hands were larger than hers.

Traffic lights beeped. Overhead, the sky had taken on the strange, curdled texture that promised snow. Cigarette butts rolled down the pavement and he tripped through the wind and ducked past preemptory umbrellas. A minute later he entered the iron doors of the austere white building that housed the library.

A minute after that, he discovered the library was closed, which was just his luck. Standing to one side, he warmed his hands against a radiator and wondered what to do next. It was still an hour and a half till the screening.

Absently, he watched a stream of elderly men milling through the entrance hall. They shuffled along, muttering to each other, wearing Berghaus jackets and carrying rucksacks and a variety of tote-bags purchased from independent bookstores. There was a lecture this evening.

Samuel followed the line towards a door marked "Council Room 37". Tacked to the wall was a sign that read:

PUBLIC LECTURE
Michael Schwarz
(University of Havel)
"Revolutions of Alfred Tarski"
17.45–18.30
Refreshments provided

The name "Tarski" rang a distant and somewhat muffled bell. He was a director, wasn't he? Sara was studying Russian Literature and Film. He checked his watch again and decided there was ample time to expand his mind on the subject of Soviet-era cinema.

On entering the room, the first thing he noticed was a long low table covered in a cloth and an array of hot beverages and biscuits. Samuel, who was still lodged in self-catering halls, prided himself on what his parents referred to as his "Communist spirit", which manifested in an unceasing search for free food. He had developed a taste for conference snacks and his eyes widened when he saw the treats on offer. The table was arrayed with selections of hazelnut-flecked cookies sprinkled with chocolate chunks and granulated sugar. There were three different types of muffin.

The other attendees collected meniscus-like around the table. Anorak rubbed against anorak as they reached for the drinks and sedimentary shortbreads. It was impressive how quickly they worked, though Samuel found the silence with which they moved a little unnerving.

A space appeared in the queue and he filled it. He felt them watching him, as he selected a ginger-nut (with crystallised ginger) and poured hot water over a bag of "Wild Berry" tea. They smiled with their eyes, and their teeth, and he felt these men were strangely pleased to see him – though he could not say exactly why. An elderly gentleman in a floppy cricket hat gave him a wink and a thumbs up.

"First time?" the cricket man asked.

Samuel nodded.

"You'll be fine," said the man.

Once the tea had been poured and the biscuits secreted in paper napkins (then in pockets and rucksacks), the attendees made their way deeper into the room where they took their seats. Samuel positioned himself by a radiator and shucked off his coat. The man in the cricket hat lowered himself onto a nearby chair.

The cricket man held up a piece of paper and tapped it lightly. At the top of the handout were the words: "Revolutions of Alfred Tarski", and the elderly man said:

"Rabbi Tarski."

Samuel smiled politely. A few minutes later, the doors at the other end of the hall swung open. There was some coughing and hushing. When the Chair walked in, it seemed to Samuel as if the room shivered. She was followed by a long man who stood beside her, hands held behind his back, heels pressed together. The Chair cleared her throat.

"Thank you, friends, for braving this miserable weather to join us. A particularly warm welcome to those of you joining us for the first time. I hope you enjoy this evening's event."

There was a smattering of applause. Overhead, fluorescent lighting cast a flat white light that glinted off the Chair's glasses. Sara wore glasses as well, with wire frames, which Samuel complimented whenever he ran out of things to say.

"I'm very pleased to welcome Professor Michael Schwarz to our Gathering. Professor Schwarz is one of the foremost historians of the logician Alfred Tarski, and of the Truth, about which he will be talking to us this evening . . ."

There was more quiet applause and the Chair retreated. Professor Schwarz stepped forward. He seemed, to Samuel, too young and too well-dressed to be a professor. He was wearing a black shirt and a black tie and sported a fashionable shading of stubble. His hair was pulled into a ponytail, bound with an elastic band, though a strand had come loose and hung winsomely across his cheek. Samuel wondered whether Sara would find this man attractive and experienced that familiar pang of jealousy.

Schwarz tapped his papers.

"As Marcia says, I am here to talk to you about the work of Alfred Tarski, and about the *Truth*. And I'm happy to see London has decided to provide an illustration of the phrase for which the man was most famous . . ."

Here, he gestured towards the window.

"*Schnee ist weiß.*"

Looking through the window, Samuel saw snowflakes falling, spiralling softly onto the pavement. It was pretty. If Sara became cold later on, he could lend her his jacket. Maybe they could go to the square and throw snowballs at each other and laugh.

"'Snow is white,'" said Schwarz. "This is the canonical sentence to which we are referred in Tarski's seminal essay 'The Semantic Conception of Truth'. 'Snow is white.' What makes this sentence true? It has something to do with snow of course. And it has something to do with *whiteness*. We need to understand our words and how they function. We need to understand how, or indeed *if* they correspond to reality. Doing so was Tarski's project. Doing so is the project with which I am engaged this evening."

Andrei Tarkovsky, thought Samuel. *Andrei Tarkovsky* was the director. *Alfred Tarski* was someone else entirely. He smiled to himself. He could tell Sara about this, he could be *ironical*. Sara loved irony (he imagined). Leaning back in his chair, he tried to think of other ironical things to say. Sara would laugh. She would glance at him shyly and their fingers would touch and their cheeks would fill with colour.

*

"In the mid-twentieth century, in a series of essays and public addresses, Alfred Tarski offered us several, now infamous, requirements for a satisfactory definition of capital-T Truth. 'Satisfactory', here means providing a usefully rigorous definition for *scientific methodology* rather than the more prosaic definition of Truth that serves for the humdrum affairs of everyday living. Among these conditions, we find the requirement that our definition not be given in the *object* language – that language under discussion – which we can call 'L' – but rather in a meta-language – let us call it 'M'. While Tarski naively assumed that these languages would be forms of higher order logic, today we like to think of 'M' as informal set theory of some description . . ."

*

Samuel blinked. He must have nodded off. It had grown stuffy in the room, and beside him the radiator hummed in tune to the fluorescent lighting. He blinked again and tried to focus on what the professor was saying. Something had slipped, and the words slid over him unpleasantly. He shook himself and sat up. The professor turned and tucked that strand of hair behind his ear. His eyes flashed like two-pence pieces.

"'. . . Snow is white' is true if and only if snow is white . . ."

The humming increased. The professor stood at the podium, pausing now and then to turn a page or reshuffle his notes. It was as if his words had begun to fold in on themselves, like the petals of a flower. Samuel felt a growing pressure behind his eyes. The radiator had started to whine – the metal juddered against the chair-leg, the chair-leg juddered against his fingers, and a mildly corrosive force began to seep through the tissues of his thoughts. Beside him, the man in the cricket hat was leaning forward, elbows on his corduroyed knees, palms cupped behind his ears to hear the speaker.

". . . The sentence 'Snow is white' is true if and only if snow exemplifies the property of whiteness, i.e. in Fregean terms, if snow falls under the concept *white* . . ."

Samuel's eyes slid around the room. Some of the other attendees were nodding, metronomically, while others had closed their eyes (whether in thought or sleep was unclear). His own eyelids were growing heavy again. He shifted in his seat. Looking at his watch he was surprised to see how little time had passed since the Chair's introduction.

Snow piled higher. He rolled his neck until it clicked, then took several deep breaths. The radiators pulsed with a heavy heat. The man in the cricket hat had bared his teeth in a simulacrum of a smile and was mouthing the words to Schwarz's lecture.

"... The phrase 'Snow is white' occurs on the left side of the equivalence in quotation marks – while on the right the sentence snow is white appears as a sentence, Snow is white, and not as the name, by which I mean 'Snow is white' . . ."

Samuel understood the form of each word, words that he himself was mouthing, but he had lost sense of their meaning. They flowed together, a strange patterning, a stream that seemed always to flow back on itself. The metal of the radiator had grown almost unbearably hot – but he found he was unable to move his leg. His limbs had grown leaden. He wondered if he should send a message to Sara, but his reserves of energy were drained by the simple act of lifting his hand to wrest his phone from his pocket. There was no signal and the clock was broken. He let it fall to the floor, where it hit the carpet with a thud that disturbed no one, least of all the professor, who was still explaining that snow was white.

Time, if that was what it was, puckered.

"I am here," said Schwarz, "to talk to you about the work of Alfred Tarski, and about the *Truth*."

He spoke with such clarity and such pin-like precision, but his words were not words that could be understood. They repeated and disappeared into each other and Samuel was faintly aware of his skin growing slack and grey. Time sagged. He felt himself slump against the window, forehead kissing the cool, damp glass.

Outside, the snow fell impossibly fast – or impossibly slowly – so slowly that each flake seemed almost to hang in the air and to catch the other snowflakes and grow. Vast, crystalline spheres spun in the void. Samuel tried to move his head, but his vision blurred. He let his pupils creep to the corners of his eyes and wondered, vaguely, why the hair on his knuckles had grown white. His nails had become scaboid and ridged, dirty, curling like snail shells.

People can go blind from staring at the snow, he thought. Someone had told him that once. It flattened space, and sitting there fixed to his chair Samuel felt the blankness expanding around him. Space had grown and all points of purchase had slipped away. That familiar grid of reference – the street, the pavement, the plane trees, the drooping lampposts – had been consumed in the cold thickness and rendered uniform.

The fluorescent lighting vibrated in the back of his head.

At the front of the room, Professor Michael Schwarz stroked his ponytail and leaned his long, elegant body across the podium. He had a power to him, an allure. This was a man Sara could not help but be drawn to. Samuel stared at those fluttering, stubbled lips. There was something horribly compelling about those ragged strips of flesh. He was reminded of that small, tidy child standing on the roadside staring in rapt fascination at the remains of the pigeon. He wished some officious parent would swoop in and guide him off to see Nana – but no parent appeared and that ragged mouth remained open.

"Snow is white," it said – which was always and inescapably true.

*

Waiting in the cinema foyer, surrounded by the smell of popcorn and pick'n'mix, Sara wondered if she'd done the right thing. It was a film, she told herself, not a contract. Maybe Samuel wanted something *other* or *more* than a friendship, but that was his problem. Fretfully, she wondered whether the intimacy of the darkened cinema might lead to unwanted knee-touching or hand-holding, and while she was annoyed that he was late – and then *very* late – she was a little relieved as well. She waited a polite twenty minutes then sent a placatory text message – "Crossed wires" – and took the Northern line home.

Her relief soured when she learned, the following day, what had happened – or rather when, like everyone else, she failed to learn what had happened. That week, she found herself explaining to Samuel's parents that yes, it seemed she had been the last person he'd contacted before he'd disappeared and no, she had no idea where he'd gone. She was required to speak to the police, to his classmates, to his lecturers. For a month she was involved in the campaigns on campus and the searches and notices on social media.

As in many such cases, however, these efforts ultimately came to nothing and four months later, Sara left London to pursue her elective in Bordeaux.

Media attention dwindled. Samuel's friends lost hope, then interest, and the events of that evening became hidden beneath a blanket of time. Eventually, despite his parents' protests, the case was consigned to the backwaters of the Metropolitan Police's over-stuffed Records Library. There, in a strip-lit office, Samuel's file was stacked in a dark corner and labelled a "cold case".

Though no one would ever know it, Samuel's file was placed alongside that of another individual who had been found the same evening of his disappearance. The body of "John Doe" was discovered by a cleaner wedged in the corner of Council Room 37. No connection was ever made between the two cases, since the first concerned a nineteen-year-old undergraduate and the second an elderly gentleman of no-fixed-abode. That the link was never made should not surprise us, since a boy does not melt into a man except over an appropriately lengthy period of time. To have identified the one with the other would have made a mockery of the relation for which Leibniz was most famous. What is true is always timelessly, implacably true – and despite any hopes for the contrary, despite the vagaries of reality, in this world snow, cold, crystalline, homoiomerous and yet not, can only ever be white.

Empty Man I: The German Logician (1902)

"Hilde close the door there is a draught a *draught* I said are you deaf
as well as stupid have you stoppered up your ears? ...take off your
jacket and your shoes I will not have you tracking snow and dogshit
into the house your mother has just cleaned it is bad enough that
you–...no no *no* give me no excuses you are alive and you are
breathing so I see no earthly reason why you should be so late–...yes
Hilde yes *yes* you are late it is well past the hour we have eaten I have
fed your supper to the dogs who have a greater respect for time-
keeping than my daughter... why are you doing that? why? why?
...do not cry do not cry I forbid you from crying I forbid it... sit
down and do not cry you will sit here yes right here with your back
straight and your arms by your sides and you will be quiet and you
will not cry... no no *no* I have told you I have told you I do not *care*
what waylaid you I do not care I do not– ...a *man*? ...what kind of
man? ...in a head-covering you say what kind of head-covering a
hood or a hat? did you see his face was it dark? ...was it dark? ...no

not the evening Hilde not the stars not the moon was his *face* dark
was he dark of complexion like the men at the market? ...well were
your eyes *open* Hilde were you dreaming heaven preserve me I have a
dotard for a child you are seven years old– eight years old and you
have already slumped into senility... well? ...so you do not know?
you cannot say whether he was dark or light and I will not say I am
surprised because I am not easily surprised by you any more... you
were waylaid by a mysterious figure emerging from the snow the mist
the forest the light of the evening star shining in his eyes how
romantic– ...be *quiet* Hilde be *quiet* I do not care if he crawled out of
the cracks in the earth or from the boles of the trees if he did not
forcibly restrain you Hilde if this man did not lay a hand upon you
then there is no excuse for this impudence– ...do not *snivel* I have
told you not to snivel and will not tell you again your tardiness is not
of this man's making but of your own– ...Margaret... Margaret... no
Margaret stop that...no Margaret no do not comfort her she deserves
no comfort do not bring her sausages she deserves them even less and
they were to be fed to the dogs... no no *no* we will not talk to her in
the morning we will talk to her *now* I do not care I do not care I do not
care if she is cold if she is cold it is of her own doing she would not be
cold if she had not being playing in the snow past the hour of
recreation if she had not been *gallivanting* with imaginary men in
skullcaps... yes he *was* imaginary and do not waste the firewood
Margaret no– ...no Margaret– ...Margaret I will not have you disrupt
the education of my child on a sentimental whim– ...yes Margaret
she *is* a child I said as much but her age has no bearing on the truth it
has no bearing on what is right or what is wrong these things are
unmoved by matters of age by matters of youth... Margaret Margaret
Margaret I tell you that you shall be quiet or you will go out Margaret
do not make me raise my voice again or I shall fetch my– ...I will I
will fetch it unless you– ... so are you finished I hope you are

finished... good... now where was I? Hilde you say there was a man so if there was a man will you tell me what passed between the two of you... speak up child speak up... speak up I cannot hear you... he *talked* to you? well I had assumed that he talked to you I did not think he simply stared at you like a mute but what did he say this mysterious stranger? ...what did he *say*? ...oh you cannot remember you surprise me Hilde you are approached by a hooded man on a winter's eve a man whose unexpected appearance has rendered you late for the third no fourth time this week and you cannot and you cannot and you cannot– ...*Margaret* I will not tell you again I do not care if I *am* scaring her she is lying to me and you know that I cannot abide lies... yes Hilde you *are* lying because you met no man in the snow this man is pure fiction he is a nonsense you were playing with the other truants by the lake as you have done before and you– ...do you contradict me Hilde? do you contradict your father? ...well you say you met a man but you cannot describe him and you cannot say what he– ...what's that? speak up speak up ...he talked to you about *my proof*? about *my proof*? a man a strange man a hooded man accosts you on a winter's evening to talk to you about my proof? a professor of logic perhaps a wandering pedlar of truth? you are compounding your crimes child and I will not suffer it... there exists no man there exists no man there is no such thing... do not lie to me Hilde do not lie you are angering me Hilde I have told you not to cry and you shall not cry there was no such man this man is an empty referent– ...*Hilde* are your lies truly not spent? wipe your face... with a *handkerchief* not your hand your mother did not raise a peasant... you are a dim echo of your brother yes your brother God rest his soul your brother would never have issued such lies as these was attentive to the sense of his sentences a quiet child and a good child a child who respected the truth who honoured his parents a child who was never late a child on whom sausages were never wasted... do you think he would be proud of you Hilde do you think your brother would be proud of these perversions of truth of sense? ...Margaret for the last time... Margaret I will not have you... Margaret I will not have you indulge her it serves no one... Margaret Margaret Margaret do not Margaret stop that she does not deserve your ministrations– ...yes she is our child... yes for all her swarthy features she is our child but as her parents as her teachers we have a responsibility to instil in her the virtues of honesty of fidelity to the truth and as her father I am honour-bound to make a judgement... Hilde I am honour-bound to make a judgement upon you– ...no keep silent I am honour-bound to make a judgement it is my duty as your father and you as my daughter you will obey... you will obey you *will*... I have decided you will go to the cellar... *yes* Hilde to the cellar you will go to the cellar... *why*? you ask me why? after everything she has said and the girl asks me why? because your father commands it... no Margaret no no *no* I will not be contradicted she *will* go to the cellar and she will take neither clock nor candle with her... *yes* Margaret she *shall* because I deem it appropriate and this is my house and these are my laws these are the laws of the– ...yes they are... I do yes I do Margaret and– ...what? ...what? ... speak up child if you have something to say speak up why must you always whisper I cannot hear you when your mouth is so twisted... for how long? for how long she says? *for how long?* I think you are bartering with me Hilde like some hook-nosed pedlar... you are bartering you wish to strike a bargain make a crooked deal but do I look like I have an interest in haggling? do I wear earlocks? for how long she says! I wonder sometimes whether you truly are my child or– ...sometimes I see very little of myself in you... your brother yes fair and bright and blue-eyed a boy who would have become a German man but this sallow yellow skin this nose of yours... yes look at it Hilde it is a hooked nose Hilde a hooked nose yes it is... so you will go to the cellar Hilde with your nasty hooked nose and your crimes and you will meditate upon them. it is not your tardiness that offends me most Hilde though it is heinous it is not your tardiness or your impudence but you have *lied* to me Hilde yes lied lied to me to your father– …stop crying stop crying stop crying if you cannot control yourself– …no Margaret no *no* I shall– …I have delivered my judgement… yes I have… you have lied to me Hilde you have lied to your father and to your poor mother and a lie cannot be expunged for even when revealed a lie persists a lie lives and thrives in time while the truth Hilde the truth which is as close to the divine as you and I will ever be the truth exists outside of time and so shall we place you outside of time as well and you will go to the cellar like your brother yes like your brother with neither clock nor candle and you will meditate on the meaning of truth and your crimes of tardiness and impudence and truancy and deceit and their temporal nature and your own temporal nature and you will consider what you have said you will consider the meaning and the gravity of what you have said and I will brook no complaints nor disagreement nor tears nor further lies nor mischief nor blubbing and if you cry in the darkness I shall not hear it and I shall only release you once you have taken to heart the real and substantive difference between infernal falsity and holy blessed truth …"

The Gravesend Institute

You'll think me a fool, but I took a stroll through Mordell Square this Tuesday last. It was a brisk April morning, a light frost upon the grass, tendrils of mist curling through the park. Not a soul to be seen. I sat on a bench for a time and looked at the space where the Gravesend Institute used to stand.

Perched there, on those flaking wooden slats, it all came flooding back: the crumbling stairwells, the rat turds, the greasy doorknobs – and Gerald, of course, dear Gerald, in all his abject glory. Sitting on that bench, I found the embers of recollections stoked, rekindled – and I remained there for a while, warming myself at memory's hearth.

It is strange to think of it now: the "Grave" as we used to call it. Those dirty yellow bricks, the hypnotic curlicues and crenellations. It is strange to think those staircases, bookcases, locked wooden cases, and all its secrets are now no more than motes hanging in the plane trees in Mordell Square. It is strange too, I suppose, to think that I had some part in its downfall – but no stranger, perhaps, than the ancient truth that all is fire, or wind, or water, or whatever it was that Heraclitus wrote in those flighty fragments of his.

It was twenty years ago that I first stood before those tar-black doors, listening to the church bells chime the hour. Eleven o'clock and the pigeons were cooing as I made my way up those worn stone steps, polished by a century of Oxfords, brogues and Derbys. Sitting on that bench, I recalled the youthful trepidation with which I first thumbed the crackling intercom. Was my hand shaking? Well it might have been. I was fresh out of university, with all the confidence engendered by seven years of academic browbeating.

It was, I suspect, through luck rather than design that I had been granted an interview for the position of Editorial Secretary at the Gravesend Institute. The invitation, written on behalf of Professor Almond Gilroy, had arrived by post. The paper was watermarked and hinted at a respectable (if not lucrative, *never* lucrative) future as an Officer of the Institute. Making my way up those helical stairs, I thought I caught a glimpse of myself one day rising to the heady heights of Editor and wielding the Director's sylvan stamp of Office. These are the flights of fancy to which the young are sometimes prone.

Reaching the fourth floor, I was greeted by a large moon-faced clock. It was handless, yet ticking ominously. Below it stood a door marked with a tarnished brass plaque that read, simply: Gravesend. I knocked, swiftly, to match the pace of my heart and the door opened. A man greeted me.

At the time I did not know he was called Gerald. Nothing about him gave me that impression. Until that point, the Geralds I had known were flimsy men in tortoiseshell spectacles. Tidy and particular. Well-heeled. This Gerald was the opposite. He wore neither spectacles nor suit, but was a good six feet tall and broad of shoulder. He was wearing ugly open-toed sandals and there was not a touch of tweed upon him.

I shan't bore you with the details of the interview itself, save to say I carried myself well enough for hands to be shaken and professional details exchanged. Professor Gilroy, an odd, stick-like creature, stood propped against a desk and left the talking to his colleague. At the time, they struck me as a pleasant pair. They laughed, dryly, and smiled. I had no inkling then of the resentments that riddled that wood-panelled room. I left with a spring in my step and expectations of gainful employ and a reputable future – if not within the academy, then not without it.

It strikes me as curious now, how relentlessly the human heart hopes.

Did I mention the bench was engraved? Across the back-rest was carved a short, incomplete sentence – and the scratched-out name of a man who, I was informed, loved the square and "all the trees and thoughts that grew within it". I noticed this as I was leaving. The hour had grown late, the bench uncomfortable, and my bladder insistent. I tucked my newspaper into the crook of my arm and set off for the station, forcing myself into a simulation of a merry gait. I believe I even managed a thin whistle as I left the square and my memories behind me.

*

I cannot tell you why exactly, but a week since my last visit I found myself back at that bowed park bench. I was passing, I suppose, and my knees are not what they once were so I entered the square, lay my newspaper across the wooden slats – to protect my trousers from the morning dew – and sat again, facing the space where the Grave no longer stands. Overhead, the plane trees swayed to their secret rhythms and once more the memories flickered, crackling with a strange and pleasant warmth.

I had thought at first that Gilroy and Gerald were a pleasant pair (I believe I said as much), but I was wrong. In the normal course of things I am a relatively astute observer of character. I am what my mother called "a watcher". In this instance, however, I had been bettered by my nerves (or my employers had made efforts to disguise the true character of the office).

The cruelty of the Grave came in different forms. Myself, I experienced it as a kind of erasure or neglect. I was the endnote to which Professor Gilroy never turned, the suppressed enthymeme, a central cog in the machine but rarely acknowledged as such except by Gerald in his kinder moments.

Gerald, by contrast, was subject to a clever kind of cruelty. It was a cruelty that hid behind compliments and lingered in the ambiguities of grammar and reference. From the moment our employer appeared in the mornings, shaking his umbrella, hanging up his flat-cap, he would begin the process of belittling that untenably large man.

"And how are you today, Gerald?"

Polite enough – except it was always clear from the vacant expression that Gilroy was never interested in the answer. And Gerald was always and only ever "Gerald", whereas Gilroy was never anything other than "Professor". Gerald's books (well-regarded by several respectable literary supplements) were referred to by Gilroy as "popular". "You have a knack for simplicity," the Professor would say – and Gerald would laugh – but every now and then I would sense a slight tensing of the jaw or a twitch at the corners of those downcast eyes.

Sitting on my bench, I thought of those compound cruelties, insubstantial in themselves, but with a cumulative power to level buildings – or one specific building. No trace of the Grave remains. Even the paving slabs that framed the coal-scuttle that led to that horrible basement have been prised up and discarded – a fact I noted on leaving the park, soggy newspaper under-arm, striding toward the station.

*

It has become something of a routine for me to take a morning turn about the square. I was there again today, too early for the dog-walkers and joggers, too late for the nightingales and foxes – and just in time to see the pale spring sun climb tentatively up the rooftops to set them alight. I took up my now usual pew, my bench, dedicated to that nameless soul, and with the mist rising from the dewy grass, I sank once again into reverie.

I was employed by the Institute as "Editorial Secretary". This title encompassed any number of roles, from tea-boy to copy-editor to impromptu coat-stand, but prime among them was executor of Gilroy's wishes. My days were largely spent collecting his spidery handwritten notes and enacting various editorial whims, accepting and rejecting submissions, and corresponding with our Publishers.

As I'm sure you know, the primary output of the Gravesend Institute, alongside its longstanding lecture series, was our journal: *The Socratic Quarterly*. You may have read it. It was a peculiar publication, a collection of musings from Gilroy's friends and former colleagues, on topics ranging from high metaphysics to sarcastic college humour. Indeed, it was the *S.Q.* that published the well-known "Campus Rumpus" series. Its author, Benedict March, an old if not good friend of my employer, was often in and out of the office (and I wonder, sometimes, whether Gilroy knew more about March's "endeavours" than he let on).

Typically, the Professor could be found in his Institute quarters, answering letters or murmuring into the telephone. He was a popular fellow – or pretended to be. He divided his time between short stints at the Institute and long sojourns at his club on the Mall, trips that left him smelling of cigar-smoke and brandy. I believe he also had a family somewhere in South London though they rarely featured in his anecdata. He would mention, in a practised offhand manner, his meetings with So-and-So and Such-and-Such, celebrated academics and high society politicos, and we would receive regular calls and visits from the likes of Theodore Barnhoffer, Paul Grover and Daniel Figgis. They would appear at the door, offer sarcastic remarks about Gerald, then disappear into Gilroy's study. The Grave averaged roughly one bottle of sherry a week.

It was during such visits that I felt most keenly for poor Gerald. He was never invited to join, and was made instead to sit outside with me. The walls in the building were paper-thin and Gilroy's voice, strident and sharp, pierced them easily. More often than not, Gerald was the subject of conversation, and the two of us would sit in unhappy silence as our employer praised him as faintly as possible. "A capable man," Gilroy would say, "not an overly anxious thinker and exceptionally good at moving filing cabinets." It was a sport, of sorts, like fox-hunting, or the plucking of wings from flies.

There I would sit at my desk, staring out of the window at the swaying plane trees, and listening to the clenching of Gerald's teeth and the snapping of pencils. In those moments, I hated Gilroy almost as much as Gerald must have done – perhaps more – since at times Gerald seemed curiously resigned to his fate. I felt the urge, more than once, to turn and offer solace, a kind word or an understanding look, but for some reason checked myself. I wonder, had I given comfort, if the conclusion to this sorry history might have been otherwise than what it was.

Sitting on my bench this morning, I thought I caught the smell of sulphur.

It is said that when the Grave's foundations were disinterred the labourers struck a gas main and the whole of Mordell Square was engulfed in a cloud of eggy gas. When the sun cracked across the rooftops this morning, I fancied I caught a whiff of it. If I did, it is all that remains of that twisted building. Gone are the stained and flaking walls. Gone the creaking pipes that troubled our caretaker's dreams.

Gone the library. Gone the stacks, vast forests of journals, supplements, calendars, piles of dust, correspondences. All gone. Most were lost in the conflagration, but the scant few that remained were scooped out by bulldozers and cranes and ground to infinitesimals – and this new building, all glass and steel, is built on solid ferroconcrete foundations, not the rotten wood that once latticed this soil.

*

My bench affords me a view inside the new university building, the one that stands tall where the Grave used to hunch. Had I the luxury of time I would stay the day and surely see, through the windows and large glass doorways, students working, secretaries typing on their clever computers. They would be young and fresh-faced – even the old ones. As it is, I see no one, not a soul, though every now and then the mists curl and I think I catch a glimpse of a familiar stoop, bent figures entering and leaving a building that is no longer there. I blink and they are gone. The former residents of 21 Mordell Square are unlikely to return.

In addition to his stiff upper lip, Gerald possessed formidable powers of recollection. These pertained, in the first instance, to the back catalogue of the *Socratic Quarterly*. I would sit at my desk, leafing through past issues of the journal in search of some obscure reference, and Gerald, dear Gerald, could all but repeat it *verbatim*. Not only did he know the dates of publication, the copyright details and the ordering of the contents, he knew often surprisingly intimate details about the authors' private lives. He knew about Barnhoffer's affairs, about the long-standing faculty feuds, about student indiscretions and about secrets too sordid for the sensitive ears of an Editorial Secretary. Gerald kept the records.

I sometimes wonder whether he remembered more about the Grave than he did about himself. The man was of indeterminate age and if his early years ever crossed his mind he never mentioned them.

He was immured in the most exhaustive and exhausting sense. What does it mean to inhabit an archive so completely? What does it mean to keep the records of an institution rather than oneself? I do not believe John Locke ever wrote on the subject, nor Butler, nor Berkeley, nor Hume, but it is of some interest to me. What does it do to a man to become so closely, almost inextricably tied to a building?

Sitting on my bench this morning, I spied another man across the square. At least, I believe it was a man. A man-like shape, bent and hooded in the spring mists, sitting on a bench very much like my own, staring, as I tend to stare, at a building not dissimilar to the one that has replaced the Grave. I waved. The man waved back, then stood and lumbered off in the direction of the station. The plane trees swayed and somewhere in the bushes a squirrel chittered. I rolled up my newspaper and departed.

*

Sometimes it feels as if I am always sitting on that bench, as if it is always morning, always misty. Mostly I am alone, but sometimes there are other men in the park, and always pigeons cooing. It is often damp. The dew, the mist, the mizzling drizzle that does not fall but rather hangs. Somehow, the tips of my socks are always wet.

My last true memory of warmth was from the night it happened. I was sitting there, on my bench, that self-same bench, while I watched the building burn. I watched the blush of fire blossom into great and beautiful flowers of flame, I watched as they spread hungrily up those ancient walls. And when the roof caved in and dark plumes of smoke issued out into the London air, I watched and I felt warm.

Gerald was alone in the office when Professor Gilroy arrived. The Professor removed his cap and offered the usual sarcastic pleasantries.

The evening's lecture had gone well and he was in good spirits – which is to say, brandy. Only Gerald knows what Gerald had been doing, but whatever it was he stopped and stood to take the man's coat. Gilroy strolled towards his office, and almost as an after-thought murmured the fateful words:

"Milk, two sugars."

What makes a heap? How many specks of dust creates a pile? What breaks a man? How many minuscule indignities can a person suffer before he snaps? The vagueness of the boundary, I think, is less important than the effect. Gerald did not boil the kettle. He did not submerge the tea-leaves, nor pour the milk, nor stir the sugar. How many granules of sugar is moot. Gerald instead descended to the library stacks and thence to the basement, to that nexus of rotten, lousy, cobwebbed wooden pillars and doused the room in alcohol.

Amazingly, Gerald was the only casualty of the conflagration which the fire department later mistakenly attributed to an electrical disjunction. The blaze moved swiftly, but not as swiftly as the caretaker who evacuated the building and half-led, half-carried an inebriated Gilroy from his steaming study to safety. Afterwards, the Professor remembered nothing of the evening's events, save for the fact that Gerald had neglected to bring him his tea and biscuits – a fact he included in the brief tribute he gave at the funeral. Nevertheless, in recognition of Gerald's long years of service, a small amount of money was extracted from the Institute's coffers and I remember now a commemorative bench was commissioned and eventually placed in the square facing the offices where Gerald had worked and lived and died. It is strange to have forgotten this. It is strange to have forgotten so much else besides. Sitting here, on the bench where I am always sitting, I wrack my brains but cannot remember where I am supposed to be, and who, and why I am wearing such ungainly open-toed sandals.

A Response to C.D. Baird's Reading of the Pitwell Phenomenon

Richard Yates

The Socratic Quarterly (October) vol. 34, no. 5

Abstract: *This paper is a response to C.D. Baird's essay "Haunting As a Transitive Relation" (this journal) and the dualistic reading of the Pitwell Phenomenon offered within it. §1 is an introduction. §2 provides an overview of Baird's position. In §3, the "Garibaldi Transcript" is critiqued. In §4, it is argued that Baird's interpretation of the Pitwell Phenomenon (hereafter "PP") is misguided. An alternative reading, grounded in a Wimsian framework, is outlined. Baird's responses are then considered in §5 and dismissed. §6 contains a conclusion.*

Keywords: Dualism, Paul Wimsey, Pitwell Phenomenon, Pineal Gland, Haunting, Objective-Subjectivism

1. Introduction

In his much-cited essay "Haunting As a Transitive Relation" (this journal), the Cambridge metaphysician C.D. Baird attempts to revive an outmoded form of substance dualism, the view that *soul* and *body* are metaphysically distinct. At the centre of his analysis is a research programme conducted by Malcolm Pitwell at the Institute of Psychical Activities. The findings of this programme were published in the IPA's annual report last year, and summarised in this journal. Briefly put, Baird holds that the phenomenon identified by Pitwell (the "Pitwell Phenomenon", hereafter "PP") is an instance of the psychic activity commonly referred to as "haunting".

About "haunting" Baird writes,

> "'Haunt' from the Middle English 'haunten' (to reside) and the Old Norman 'hanter' (to frequent) is an activity purportedly engaged in by disembodied souls. The haunting relation is one in which one such soul affixes – or as *per* a telling cognate 'houses' – itself somewhere else..." (p. 3)

Baird states that "despite a brief and unpropitious turn towards materialism, the dualist's thesis is now very much back in fashion" (p. 3). He claims that this is "a fact to be celebrated" (p. 3). He argues, moreover, that the phenomenon identified by Pitwell – clearly articulated in the so-called "Garibaldi Transcript" – gives insight into "clandestine movements of the immaterial realm". The aim of this paper is to expose the weaknesses in Baird's account and to offer an alternative interpretation of PP removed from the problematics of classic dualism.

2. C.D. Baird's Reading of the Pitwell Phenomenon

2a. General Claims

As Baird sees it, Pitwell's findings support two general claims.

(i) *The phenomenon is considerably more widespread than previously believed.* "The evidence gathered by Pitwell and his team suggests that as many as one in four people is subject to a singular 'visitation', 'haunting' or 'housing' *per annum*." (p. 5)

(ii) *The majority (if not all) of cases involve some human individual.* "It has been previously assumed that souls were connected to geographical locations rather than people (hence 'house'). Pitwell's work suggests instead that architecture has little to no relevance in matters of spiritual residence." (p. 5)

There is little new in Baird's reading here. With respect to (i), Pitwell himself is explicitly drawing on work done by Jerricks and Ball, who are themselves inclined to think that as many as one in three people in Britain experience some form of "disturbance" every year. Baird, writing in a parenthetical aside, refers to anecdotal evidence suggesting it may be "higher still" (p. 6). This is irrelevant to the present discussion.

With respect to (ii), readers familiar with the debate may see little more than a reiteration of Geoffrey Hancock's "Soul-Body-Soul" thesis (see his article of the same name in this journal). However, Baird takes pains to identify his own "dramatic innovations". He writes:

"My own analysis departs from Hancock's in two important particulars. In the first instance, I have offered an historical analysis of the phenomenon, which focuses on the Cartesian hypothesis that the soul interacts with the body via the *pineal gland* (I explore this further in my 'Corporeal Tethers', this journal). To my mind, Hancock's account overlaps with the Cartesian hypothesis, and is supported by Pitwell's findings. The pineal gland may well serve as the material conduit for *other* spirits (hence 'Soul-Body-Soul')... This, certainly, is more persuasive a thought than the competing notion that spirits may stand in the haunting relation to inanimate non-psychic masses, such as religious sites or 'haunted houses' (a tautology if ever there was one)... Secondly, in contrast to Hancock, I have contended that *the body is an accidental part of the haunting relation*." (p.23)

This claim, that the body is "an accidental part of the haunting relation", is the foundation of what Baird refers to as his "Soul–Soul" thesis (hereafter "SS"). Discussed in the next section, SS holds that "souls can tether to other souls, realised in material form or not" (p. 13).

2b. SS and Philosophical Disagreement

In §3 of his essay, Baird formalises SS as follows:

SS: "*One immaterial substance can connect with another immaterial substance without a material intermediary.*" (p. 19)

In §4, he cites this present paper and goes on to say:

"If souls attach to other souls, rather than physical bodies or geographical locations, the mechanism by which they do so is, despite Yates's claims to the contrary, frustratingly obscure... Pitwell's findings, however, offer a variety of avenues for further inquiry. The one I am most inclined to explore concerns something I will designate the 'Disagreement Function'...

...It has long been supposed that hauntings occur around sites of psychic trauma (see e.g. Hopkirk's 'Psychological Disturbances', this journal), and amongst these events, 'grievances' or 'grudges' are the most common. Issues of debts unpaid, wrongs uncorrected and crimes unpunished abound..." (p. 21)

The arguments in this section are convoluted, but Baird appears to be claiming that disagreements, particularly persistent ones, generate substantial connections *between* "immaterial substances". In §6, he formalises this claim as follows:

DF: "*A soul can (and often does) connect to other such entities through a process of disagreement (as yet unexamined).*" (p.32)

He goes on to argue that a corollary of SS is that "one disembodied soul may stand in the haunting relation to *another* disembodied soul" (p. 31). It is logically possible "for a ghost to haunt another ghost" (p. 33). In Baird's view, it is plausible that there are "linked chains of souls, each one standing in a haunting relation to the next" (p. 34).

This raises the question implicit in the title of his essay: is haunting a transitive relation? That is, if soul A haunts soul B, and soul B haunts soul C, does soul A haunt soul C? Baird responds in the affirmative, grounding his answer in his analysis of the Disagreement Function (DF). In §7, he refers to work by Mulvey and Bracken,

"...who have shown with great lucidity that many common-or-garden disagreements are *dyadic* in nature. Richard disagrees with Charlie's adultery. Charlie disagrees with Richard's moralism. Their disagreement does not extend beyond this two-person relationship. However, there are other forms of disagreement that "carry". To quote further from Mulvey and Bracken:

'Consider the *family feud*, in which participants disagree in virtue of group membership. My grandfather disagreed with your grandfather, my father with yours on the same grounds, I disagree with you for identical reasons, and our children shall do the same...'

I have noticed that, when it comes to the phenomenon under discussion, psychic connections have been reported to follow very similar lineages. With great regularity, we are told of descendants being haunted by the victims of an ancestor's transgressions..."
(pp. 32–33)

Based on Mulvey and Bracken's analysis, Baird argues that "philosophical conflicts" should be added to the class of "persisting disagreements". He claims that the historical data shows "few grievances are so long held, or so easily carried, as those that concern matters of philosophical doctrine" (p. 35). In particular, he focuses on the debate between materialists and dualists, writing that "the disagreement over mind and body has persisted, nay *raged*, for centuries if not millennia" (p. 36). This leads to what he calls the "Psycho-Philosophical Chain thesis" (PPC):

PPC: "*Philosophical disagreements ground psychic chains of interconnected souls*" (p. 38)

PPC then leads to "a dramatically new methodological approach" (p. 39), which Baird calls "Transitive Historical Analysis" (p. 39), to be considered in the sub-section below.

2c. Transitive Historical Analysis

In the second half of his essay, Baird considers what he sees to be a fundamental problem "which has long dogged the efforts of researchers such as Pitwell" (p. 40):

"While consensus grows that the pineal gland (or a related organic substrate) is merely an *accidental* conduit by which souls communicate with other souls, the body remains frustratingly central to psychic congress. When communing with spirits, it is always via a physical intermediary (see Kepler's list of techniques in his 'Teller's Litany', this journal). It is a matter of great frustration to have these research efforts so confounded – and it is likewise perilously easy to fall foul of a verificationist critique..." (p. 41)

As Baird sees it, SS cannot effectively be tested if any test necessarily involves a physical intermediary. To combat this problem, he offers a new methodological approach. His "Transitive Historical Analysis" (THA), emerges out of his analysis of SS, DF and PPC:

"If we follow the above reasoning, we are lead to an alluring methodological prospect. Where seers were once seen to commune with single souls, the possibility now arises that they may access long chains of interconnected psychic substances. Where philosophical disagreement persists, a seer may theoretically approach a member of a certain school (a materialist, for instance) and thereby engage with parallel stands of dualist/materialist interlocutors..." (pp. 41–42)

According to Baird, SS can be examined by a single intermediary who engages with a "chain". Moreover, Baird states that this chain can offer the intermediary access to historically distant "souls" as well as those directly "haunting" a subject or subjects. By this means, he claims, deep historical analysis can be conducted. In the remainder of this paper, Baird's interpretation of the Garibaldi manuscript will be challenged and an alternative reading will be outlined.

3. Reports of the Pitwell Phenomenon

The keystone of Baird's analysis is the transcript of the event produced by Pitwell and his team. The so-called "Garibaldi transcript" contains an exchange and a description of Master Garibaldi's experience. The notes were recorded by the Institute's stenographer, who is referred to only as "J.N.". Pitwell writes that the session was closed and conducted in accordance with the Institute's Code of Conduct. The exchange is reprinted in full in Baird's article and consists of Master Garibaldi asking a series of pre-prepared questions and receiving answers. Some of these answers are less germane than others. For instance,

> "*Garibaldi*: Is it true that the pineal gland is accidental to the process of spiritual communion?
> *Respondent*: She is burning, always burning. . ." (p. 34)

> "*Garibaldi*: Can you tell me how far back the line stretches?
> *Respondent*: It is so bitterly cold, but she is so hot, a fire that burned, a fever made flesh. . ." (p. 41)

For present purposes, the dialogue is less important than Garibaldi's description of the experience. Baird writes:

> "Master Garibaldi's description of the experience is, I think, of considerable significance here. It is, as the reader will surely agree, compelling evidence to support the Soul–Soul thesis I have advanced above. Master Garibaldi's statement runs as follows,
>
> 'Upon entering my trance, I, myself, the Seer Garibaldi, was immediately thrown into a beautiful confusion of sharp colours and hot smells. . . Additionally, I was confronted with a wonderful snaking line of faces, talking radiantly to one another but all the while looking at me. . . Every time I would ask a question, they would converse and words of disagreement would ripple up and

down the snake and eventually the largest face, the face closest to me, would reply. This was how our conversation progressed and yes, every word spoken in that realm is now indelibly and joyfully burned in my heart. . .'

Garibaldi's 'line of faces', I contend, is a helical chain of interconnected psychic substances. These are the long-dead (well-named) in conversation, soul talking to soul, talking to soul, talking to soul. . ." (pp. 38–39)

In fact, there is little in the dialogue to substantiate Baird's reading. The "respondent" avoids questions about the nature of their communication and answers either non-sequitorally, enigmatically or with tautologies. Baird's SS appears to stand or fall with this interpretation of Garibaldi's description. Garibaldi – "a well-respected practitioner" (p. 42) – states he saw a "line of faces", apparently in conversation with each other. They trade "words of disagreement" (in support of DF). On these grounds, Baird suggests THA is exemplified by exchanges such as the following:

"*Garibaldi*: What was the state of the world in your age?
Respondent: Wet." (p. 44)

4. Reappraisal of the Pitwell Phenomenon

While Baird's dualistic analysis of the Garibaldi Transcript is initially plausible, it neglects discussions around the limits of conceptual schema. In the remainder of this paper, Paul Wimsey's "objective-subjectivism" will be articulated and shown to provide a simpler and richer explanation of Garibaldi's report. The necessity of doing so is clear from the comments in Baird's essay about this essay, which demonstrate a lack of understanding about current trends in metaphysics (e.g. "Yates's whimsical objective-subjectivism is gutter-snipe relativism without the charm..." (p. 54)).

4a. Objective-subjectivism

Paul Wimsey's paper "Objective-subjectivism" has been the subject of considerable commentary and debate (see e.g. Yates's "Objects and Subjects in Wimsey's Objective-Subjectivism", this journal). Its critics see it as an unwelcome return to stagnant conversations about "noumena" and "things-in-themselves". Others – including Daniel Figgis, Andrew O'Connor and Benjamin Sallow – see it as providing a generative metaphysical framework that complements rather than collides with the analytic method. Whatever its failings, it provides a helpful alternative to the brute substance dualism advocated by Baird.

For the Objective-Subjectivist, reality (the world, the universe) is fully independent of human thought. There is no lingering relativism in Wimsey's account. However, while the world is not wholly determined by the human mind, nor is it "self-articulating". That is, the human mind has a primary role to play in individuation. Humans possess specific conceptual schema, which capture certain entities and (putatively) neglect others. Metaphysics is always human metaphysics and the objective objects of reality are always subjectively determined by the human subject.

One question, which has become increasingly prominent in discussions around OS, is the extent to which the human schema might change. If change were a possibility, a further question arises: What new entities might it learn to individuate?

4b. Garibaldi's "Line of Faces"

Consider again Garibaldi's "line of faces".

> "I was confronted with a wonderful snaking line of faces, talking radiantly to one another but all the while looking at me..." (p. 38)

> "Words of disagreement would ripple up and down the snake..." (p. 39)

On Baird's interpretation, Garibaldi is confronted by a long line of metaphysically distinct "souls in conversation" – or, as he refers to it later, "a winding celestial queue" (p. 46). This makes sense within a tradition of dualistic thinking in which immaterial substances are "ghosts", wandering around, spatially discrete and able to "disagree" with one another.

There is no reason to prefer this implicitly religious metaphysics to the simpler and more elegant picture provided by OS. A Wimsian will read Garibaldi's statement as a description of an entity that normally escapes the human's conceptual schema. It is no accident that Garibaldi refers to the line of faces, on two occasions, as "snake-like". The implication is that the "faces" are in fact part of a larger whole. The synaesthetic "sharp colours" and "hot smells" also suggest a deviation from the "normal" categories of thought – and the apparent non-sequiturs that populate the exchange indicate a failure of translation from one system to another. Baird's account sees the Pitwell Phenomenon as a case of spiritual communion, with a living person (Garibaldi) talking to a series of "souls". In order to substantiate this claim, Baird invokes a variety of increasingly convoluted theses

(SS, DF, PPC). PP, however, can be more simply explained by reference to OS. Garibaldi does not "talk to ghosts". His conceptual scheme latches onto entities that otherwise fall between the categories of human thought.

5. A Response to Baird's Response

The argument above rests on a preference for ontological parsimony, the view that when it comes to metaphysics *simpler is better*. Citing this present essay, Baird writes in his own:

> "Yates, like his iniquitous forefathers, has a taste for desert landscapes. He claims (and note well the unnecessary acronyms!):
> '...PP can be more simply explained by reference to OS...'
> Like many of today's younger metaphysicians, Yates also has a cool disregard for what he sees to be work that is 'implicitly religious'. 'There is no reason to prefer this implicitly religious metaphysics to the simpler and more elegant picture provided by OS.' What he curiously neglects is the extent to which his own metaphysical judgements are in fact aesthetic declarations – an issue, perhaps, particular to anyone as enamoured as he is with 'OS'..." (p. 51)

Baird's suggests: (i) that simplicity is an aesthetic rather than a formal issue in metaphysics and (ii) that appeals to ontological parsimony are conceptually equivalent to appeals to the posits of religious frameworks. In response to (i), it can be noted, as a matter of historical record, that there are no successful scientific theories which multiply entities beyond necessity (for more on this, see Benwell's "Simple Science", this journal).

With respect to (ii), it is worth noting that Baird's own reading of the Garibaldi Transcript fails to align with the Christologically informed dualism he believes is under attack from "today's younger metaphysicians". There is no mention of anything even vaguely resembling a "winding celestial queue" in the canonical texts of the Soul-Body religions. His reading of the Garibaldi Transcript is more iconoclastic than the Wimsian interpretation, which makes no claims about the reality of "souls".

Towards the end of his essay, Baird offers a conciliatory note about the words currently being written:

> "Of course, Yates is right to (re)emphasise the importance of the Garibaldi manuscript – and much could be gained from an interview with our spiritual intermediary. The concept of 'second-sight' is multiply interpretable, but closer conversation with a Seer, especially one as eloquent as Master Garibaldi, would be undeniably useful and may help us determine whether what he sees are souls (as per my interpretation) or entities from an orthogonal reality (as per Yates's)..." (p. 66)

Baird is correct and it is unfortunate that there is so little information about the intermediary known as "Garibaldi". The Institute of Psychical Activity has authenticated his credentials and stated that he was among their "most successful" practitioners. It is a matter of some frustration that the intermediary has disaffiliated from the Institute and changed addresses, but it is hoped that at some point in the future, contact will be made and, as Baird puts it, these outstanding issues can be "laid finally and happily to rest".

6. Conclusion

In §1, the debate around the Pitwell Phenomenon (PP) was introduced. In §2, Baird's analysis was articulated and the Soul-Body-Soul thesis

(SBS), the Soul–Soul thesis (SS), the Disagreement Function (DF), the Psycho-Philosophical Chain thesis (PPC) and the notion of Transitive Historical Analysis (THA) were explained. In §3, it was shown that Baird's analysis relies heavily on a certain section of the Garibaldi Transcript, specifically Garibaldi's description of a "line of faces" and souls "in conversation". In §4, an alternative reading of this description was offered, in line with Wimsey's objective-subjectivism (OS). In §5, Baird's response to this re-description was considered and responded to. §6 is this present conclusion.

It is worth noting that Baird's analysis is correct in one important regard. The debate between the materialists and the dualists has been "long-running, and seemed at times circular". Baird's essay perpetuates this problem. By engaging with Wimsey's Objective-Subjectivism, the present paper attempts to draw it to a close.

Bibliography

Baird, C.D., "Haunting As a Transitive Relation", this journal, (October) vol. 34, no. 5

Baird, C.D., "Corporeal Tethers", this journal, (October) vol. 34, no. 5

Benwell, R., "Simple Science", this journal, (October) vol. 34, no. 5

Hancock, G., "Soul-Body-Soul", this journal, (October) vol. 34, no. 5

Hopkirk, R., "Psychological Disturbances", this journal, (October) vol. 34, no. 5

Jerricks, T. & Ball, S., "Recent Survey of 'Psychic Disturbances' in England and Wales", this journal, (October) vol. 34, no. 5

Kepler, S., "Teller's Litany", this journal, (October) vol. 34, no. 5

Mulvey, R. & Bracken, B., "An Argument for Persistent Disagreement", this journal, (October) vol. 34, no. 5

Pitwell et al., "The Garibaldi Transcript", this journal, (October) vol. 34, no. 5

Wimsey, P., "Objective-Subjectivism", this journal, (October) vol. 34, no. 5

Yates, R., "Objects and Subjects in Wimsey's Objective-Subjectivism", this journal, (October) vol. 34, no. 5

Yates, R., "A Response to C.D. Baird's Reading of the Pitwell Phenomenon", this journal, (October) vol. 34, no. 5

Empty Man II: Theodore (1999)

"just calm down take a breath... no I didn't say *irrational*... no I may have *thought* it but I didn't *say* it... no no actually I *am* taking this seriously... do I have to shout to show I'm taking it seriously? yes you *are* shouting that constitutes shouting in a library... what do you mean you find it *infuriating*? I'm just talking the way I normally talk ...I'm sorry if it's too *measured* for you would you rather I was more hys– no don't interrupt me I was going to say *histrionic* not hysterical... all I mean is I prefer not to make a public scene... yes the *public* library is a *public* building... yes there *is* someone around you said yourself you saw a man by the yes the man with the hood– ...look I've told you I don't like shouting and I find it upsetting that you think you can just *emote* at me... *yes* upsetting we're adults we can talk things through rationally ...no I didn't say you were being irrational you *inferred* that... why can't you just listen to what I'm saying? you lot are all the same and no before you say anything I don't mean women I mean literature students just calm down will you take a breath... no I'm trying to be helpful it's a suggestion yes I *realise* you were going to take a breath anyway I'm not an idiot but you need to calm down or you'll hyperventilate if you'll let me explain no let me finish you can't keep talking over me... yes I *am* going to say it's disrespectful because it *is* disrespectful... well if you act like a child I'm going to talk to you like a child you can't just *express* at me... adults talk and reason together with the aim of reaching a mutual understanding... well I'm sorry you think I'm being pompous because personally I think I'm being sensible do you think I like being the grown-up all the time? no stop shouting at me it's not like you've never made a mistake in your life–...stop shouting stop shouting stop shouting stop shouting stop shouting stop shouting stop shouting stop shouting... thank you as I was saying it's not like you've never made a mistake in your life... yes it *was* a mistake actually a mistake yes I wasn't being vindictive was I? ... no I'm not being sarcastic because sarcasm involves a contortion of the truth and of course I didn't want to hurt you... yes I know I *did* I can see that I did but that wasn't my *intention* there's a world of difference between doing something and *intending* to do something... no no *no* it's not just semantics nothing's *just* semantics... semantics are important because semantics are how we communicate with each other not by shouting... no I'm just trying to be *precise*... because otherwise we won't get anywhere will we? we'll go around in circles... no I'm *not* I'm not trying to confuse you I'm doing the exact opposite I'm trying to bring some *clarity* to the situation... listen it was a mistake and I'm sorry it hurt you... yes that's what I said... a propositional sentence. I'm sorry *that* it hurt you... you wanted me to say I'm sorry and I'm saying I'm sorry that it hurt you... no this isn't a game to me. I'm sorry *that* it hurt you but I'm not sorry because of what I did because it was a mistake and I didn't do it on purpose and if I didn't do it on purpose than I'm not responsible so I can't be sorry for it... well actually that's how responsibility works in england– ...yes I said england what's wrong with that I said it because that's what I meant. I'm not talking about the united kingdom I don't know how the law works in wales and no

I'm not being *racist* can we please stay on topic. . . no I'm *not* treating you like one of my foreign students and I resent the implication. . . in england responsibility is apportioned based on intent and I didn't *intend* to hurt you I made a mistake. . . .of course I regret it of course. . . for one thing I regret how angry you are. . . well actually I'm *not* being facetious I genuinely regret how angry you are it's upsetting. I'm upset that you can't see I'm upset. . . I think we're getting off topic– . . .no don't shout stop shouting okay you're angry I can see you're angry I can hear that you're angry everybody in a ten-mile radius can hear that you're angry I just want to know if you think you have a right to be angry. . . well no in fact I don't no. . . because you're being *hypocritical* because you've made mistakes as well. . . for one thing you lost my favourite– . . .yes I *am* bringing that up because it's relevant it was my favourite– . . . stop talking over me stop it stop it stop talking over me it was my favourite and I miss it but I recovered. . . what do you mean it's not the same thing of course it's not the same thing because we didn't make *identical* mistakes because that would be physically if not logically impossible. . . it's a *comparable case*. . . you made a mistake and I got over it and I made a mistake so. . . yes I recognise there are varying degrees but both are still mistakes and if I didn't *mean* to do it if I didn't *intend* to do it then it's not really fair you treating me like this. . . like *this* like all of *this*. . . I'm gesturing because I don't want to be rude. . . okay okay. . . crying really isn't going to solve anything is it? what would you do if *I* started crying if I sat down beside you and started bawling my eyes out? . . .yes actually I *do* know how to cry I'm just more restrained than you are. . . no did I *say* that? did I? did those words come out of my mouth? no but for the record there's a reason someone coined the term crocodile tears. . . yes yes there is– . . . oh really? . . .according to your interpretation of– . . .next you'll be accusing me of calling you a crocodile. . . all I'm saying is that your crying isn't helping we've had a disagreement we have different opinions and we need to achieve some *reflective equilibrium* and crying isn't helping us do that you think my mistake was worse than your mistake and I'm saying both are mistakes and neither were intentional and isn't that what matters? …yes it *was* a mistake I thought we'd established that… it was a mistake an error of judgement I was *mistaken* in thinking it was okay… oh really? *really?* are you saying I *wasn't* mistaken in thinking it was okay? well firstly you're presuming to know my own mind better than I do which is something I've been criticised for doing in the past and secondly if you agree that I *was* mistaken then you also think I made a mistake… you made a mistake and I made a mistake– …pardon? …actually I think you mean *equivocating* the word is *equivocating*… no I'm not patronising you I'm just saying you used the wrong word… I don't understand …do you really think shouting is going to help me understand better? stop shouting stop shouting stop shouting stop shouting stop shouting stop shouting… no I'm not how am I getting aggressive when I'm talking quietly if anyone's aggressing anyone it's you you're aggressing my ears you're aggressing the ears of the man in the– …how is *logic* aggressive? is this what they teach you over there? …no I'm not using a *tone*… I'm not… this is besides the point… no that's irrelevant that's irrelevant that's irrelevant I'm not being disparaging at all I have a lot of friends in the literature department… like Alan… Alan… *Alan*… yes Professor Jackson yes we're friendly if you're friendly with someone you're friends and anyway this is irrelevant what's relevant is that I recognise I made a mistake and I'm sorry that it upset you what more do you want? …I don't know why you're getting so worked up about it she was just a student… no no no no you're inferring again… I *realise* you're a student but that's not the point the point is that it didn't mean anything it was utterly inconsequential… no I'm not– …no I'm not minimising anything… well how can you *see* what I'm doing when I'm not *doing* anything? you can't see something that isn't there and before you say anything no I'm not suggesting you're *imagining* it because I know where that leads and heaven forbid I suggest a student of english literature might have an active imagination... I'm just trying to be reasonable you're shouting at me and crying and calling me names and all I'm doing is talking talking that's all I'm not doing anything *sinister* it's not some great *conspiracy* my words are just words that's all they are I'm just trying to be calm and considered and mature... yes *mature* it's what's supposed to happen when you grow up... can you please stop shouting stop shouting stop shouting... if you'll let me finish I'll explain if you'll let me finish if you'll... thank you as I was saying it was *inconsequential* it meant *nothing* but yes I agree it was an error of judgement a mistake... there you see we're agreeing this is how adults deal with arguments... progress... well no just because I said I made a mistake doesn't mean everything she said is true that doesn't follow you're inferring again... you have a very Humean understanding of inference ...as it happens very little of what she said is true except for the fact that she correctly reported my name and correctly identified me as her lecturer... yes I *am* denying it... no I'm not going to go into the details of the all things I'm denying or we'd be here for ever I'm denying *it* and frankly I'm a little upset that you don't believe me... upset yes would you like me to demonstrate by sitting down there and crying next to you or will you take me at my word? ...calm down calm down calm down calm down... look all I'm asking for is a little consistency that's all if I can get over your mistake you can get over mine– I beg your pardon? ...what do you mean *a general attitude*? I don't know what you mean an attitude what kind of attitude? ...I'm not being obtuse I'm just asking a question a reasonable question... so me being reasonable is an attitude and you're saying that's a bad thing? well I think this is a digression but why don't you explain it to me? why don't you explain it to me? I'm asking you to explain it to me

...no I won't pick at you... so you're saying that being calm and considered is an attitude and that's a bad thing well I'm just asking that you abide by the strictures of logic ...well I mean that I'd like it if you were minimally consistent... consistent... consistent yes... stop shouting stop shouting stop shouting... yes you *are* shouting if I can hear you talking in a library you're shouting... stop it stop shouting stop shouting stop shouting stop shouting just stop stop stop stop stop stop... no I'm not I'm not doing that at all–... well I will if you stop shouting I'll stop– ...stop shouting stop shouting stop shouting stop shouting stop shouting stop shouting.... okay okay okay there okay that's better that's much better I don't know why you have to make such a fuss there's never a reason to make such a fuss especially in a library this is a place of learning.

Bare Substrata

The realist believes that the world exists in every way independent of human thought. A stone is a stone is a stone and no amount of thinking will make it otherwise. The conceptualist, by contrast, believes the world is a construct, lying some way causally downstream of the minds that perceive it. There are few philosophers who wholeheartedly endorse either position; most hover some way between the two, believing that while the universe exists – come what may – it is not unchanged by the angling of the human mind. Professor Daniel Figgis was the subtlest and most competent of these hoverers, and his book *Individuating Items* contains perhaps the clearest articulation of his Realist-Conceptualism – the view, as he put it, that the human mind brings something to the table, though the table exists regardless.

It was this book, *Individuating Items*, that Charlie clasped to his delicate chest as he skittered down the staircase to the basement room of his central London college. His was a dog-eared token of the type, pages browned, margins besmirched, spine cracked and broken. Figgis had, for the last two years, been the focus of his doctoral studies – but due to both social and academic anxiety, this was Charlie's first outing to the Figgis Reading Group.

His experience of such groups was minimal. He found them unwelcoming, cliquey, populated by taut, tall men who made in-jokes and scrawled overzealously on whiteboards. He was nervous and his mother's suggested remedy had been to bake a tray of blueberry muffins, which were presently misting the inside of the tupperware within his rucksack. "Everyone likes a blueberry muffin," Helen had said, "and people talk less with their mouths full." His mother's mind worked according to a logic that Charlie admired, but did not always understand.

Passing piles of shipping boxes and rows of dead pot-plants, he made his way down the corridor. The signs, typically, pointed in contradictory directions, but finally, temples moist, glasses steamed, he found himself in front of an unremarkable red door marked "BR3". He paused and listened. He heard a voice, stentorian, coming from the other side.

Taking a deep breath, he knocked. The voice continued. When he knocked again and the voice stopped, he tentatively opened the door. Inside, he discovered a group of blinking men, hunched at a low table.

"Is this. . . is this the Figgis reading group?"

The tallest of the four men nodded. "And you are?"

"Charlie." He waved his copy of *Individuating Items*.

The room was small, white and poorly lit. Its walls were lined with shelves of numbered box files and the odd stack of papers. Charlie wiped the sweat from his upper lip and edged his way inside. The men watched impassively as he shuffled into a chair and out of his jacket. He left the cakes in his bag – it seemed childish now to have brought them – and instead opened *Individuating Items* at random. He began writing nothings in the margins, hoping his neighbour, an angular man with a painfully sharp Adam's apple, wouldn't study them too closely.

not really now, he wrote,
between the possibility of seeing and not seeing
ereuthophobia

Ignoring Charlie, the angular man continued what he'd been saying,

"It's a sham. It's analytic posturing."

Beside a browning spider-plant, another of the students shook his head. "Excuse me, Chair, I disagree–"

"He's describing *the structure of human experience*," the angular man barked. "It's a completely different kettle of fish."

"Category mistake! It's exactly the same kettle of fish."

The four men had clearly already forgotten Charlie. He surveyed them over the top of his book. Clockwise from his left sat: a man with a noncommittal smile; the head-shaker; . . .some inexplicable *x*; and, sitting directly to his right, the angular man, who appeared to be composed almost exclusively of elbows.

Charlie could feel the warmth of the cakes in his rucksack. He imagined the inside of the tupperware beading with sweat and the thought made him both nauseous and slightly ashamed. He should never have listened to Helen. Blueberry muffins.

The angular man turned to the empty seat.

"Chair," he said, "I know what Figgis *says* he's doing, but he's wrong–"

"Chair," interrupted the man with the noncommittal smile, "I object. Figgis explicitly states–"

"Thing," said the head-shaker, "the structure of the human mind is a guide to the structure of reality *if and only if* the structure of reality is dependent on the structure of the human mind."

"Idealism," said the noncommittal smile.

The angular man sighed.

"Idealism is not a tenable philosophical position."

Charlie stared into the seams of his book and found a hair lodged in the gutter. He blew it away. It was true that idealism was an unattractive philosophical prospect – and it was also true that idealism was compatible with the descriptivism found in *Individuating Items*.

But Figgis looked to the human mind as a guide to metaphysical inquiry, not because he thought the world mind-dependent, but because the mind developed in response to the world. He thumbed through the book, found the relevant passage, and prepared himself.

The men continued to ignore him. Their gazes rested thoughtfully on the disturbingly empty chair at the corner of the table. The angular man had started nodding again, running a hand through his thinning hair. Charlie cleared his throat. No one seemed to hear him. He decided to underline the passage in his book, once, twice, three times. Beside him, the angular man began to murmur.

"I was thinking, Thing, that while idealism requires a degree of descriptivism, the converse is not necessarily true. The mind need not construct reality. It simply *construes* it in a certain way."

The head-shaker nodded. "Conceptual frameworks respond to the exigencies of reality."

"And anyway," the angular man continued, "metaphysics must attend to human experience."

This was precisely why Charlie avoided these reading groups. Despite claims to the contrary, they were closed, static things. They did not lose or gain new parts. They were fragile aggregates, constituted by self-important men who said self-important things. He let his book fold closed and let his gaze drift to the empty chair that seemed to be garnering so much more attention than he was.

It was one of the many blue plastic-backed chairs that lived in such basements, flecked with paint and badly scuffed around the ankles. It was the kind of chair that bowed dangerously when you leaned on it, as much at home in a classroom as a church hall as a town hall as a skip. It was an ordinary chair, and yet it seemed curiously *present*. He found his eyes slipping over it, towards its neighbours and the shelves behind it, where the box files stood to attention. Charlie frowned and tried to refocus. *Strange*, he thought. It was ludicrous to think of chairs as attentive – to think of chairs as anything at all – yet attentive is how it somehow seemed.

He was being ridiculous. He was irritated by these pompous men, and the wasted muffins and the condensation dripping down the sides of the tupperware in his rucksack. He was irritated at his mother for having told him to bake them, and at himself for having listened. He was irritated by his own nervousness, by the sweat on his upper lip. It was an empty chair, that was all. And if these men looked at it and smirked occasionally, it meant nothing. It was all part of their silly game.

"Chair!" barked the angular man. "Scientific inquiry is an obvious contender."

"Science is a human practice," retorted the head-shaker.

The angular man smirked. "Thing, I'm sure the Chair will agree that the boiling point of water is not chosen by committee."

Charlie's gaze flitted back to the empty space. The chair. Blue, paint-flecked and bowing. There was a man sitting in it.

He had been there all along, of course. Charlie had seen him – though he had wished, quite desperately, that he hadn't. There was not anything obviously malignant about this man, who was dowdy and wore a simple starched white collar and austere black jacket – but there was something uncanny in that heavy panting. When he moved to turn the pages of his book or to look at the students, he did so with a curious, forced precision. Every now and then he would cross his hooded eyes with a hand and sigh. His tongue was grey and covered in prominent villi.

Charlie looked away, but now found his gaze crawling helplessly back. On the table in front of the man lay an older, or earlier, version of *Individuating Items* and the man licked his papery lips and turned another page. They were mundane gestures, yet each one sent a shiver down Charlie's back and arms and throat. He tried again to look away, but couldn't.

The man was both there and not there. Or rather, the space where he sat, on that blue and empty chair, teemed with presence and absence, to which Charlie found he could not but attend. There was the man, pale and blinking and he overlapped somehow with a lump of flesh. Minuscule worms wove a curling vermiculation through puffy red tissues, tissues that shimmered across the surface of a grey sludge. Beneath that sludge – or on top of it – lay a nothing, a thick emptiness that burrowed into Charlie, while in his rucksack, in his tupperware, his muffins steamed and seeped.

Was he screaming? If he was, the others were oblivious to it. Maybe his screams registered on a level beyond their hearing, like the calls of bats, or the lowing of whales. He tried to close his eyes, but found he couldn't. The empty man had turned to him, a quizzical twist to those dry, tight lips, lips which were flesh and yet not. How could the two be identical when they were so dramatically different? It was a puzzle that not even the "is" of constitution could resolve. Yes, thought Charlie, he was screaming, he was sure of it now. Or laughing. A hideous, clicking, polyphonic laugh.

In his rucksack, the muffins grew damper. The greaseproof paper peeled, the sponge grew stodgy and weak. The blueberries worked themselves free of the cake and rolled to the base of the box. Charlie remembered how, as a boy, his mother had stood with him at the kitchen and explained the recipe. The ingredients, (1) flour, (2) eggs, (3) sugar, (4) blueberries and (5) . . .

The empty man's lips moved, but Charlie heard no discernible words. The other students nodded vigorously. The man with the noncommittal smile was no longer smiling, but rubbing the heels of his hands into his eye sockets, as if trying to push through to the other side. The empty man shuffled in his empty chair, and stared at Charlie. Charlie tried desperately to focus instead on:

(1) the memory of his mother, Helen;

(2) the fact that muffins are something over and above their ingredients;

(3) ...;

(4) the belief that sound travels infinitely,

(5) the belief that there is no silence, just an endless, throbbing background hum;

(6) ...;

(7) anything but that pale and empty man;

(8) anything but those dry and calcified lips;

(9) the statement: There does not exist some man;

(10) the statement: There does not exist some man with an outstretched arm;

(11) the statement: There does not exist some man whose fingers are enclosing my own.

*

Professor Daniel Figgis and those who followed him, held that there are things to which we must attend if we are to navigate the world in the way that we do. These are the substances, those day-to-day objects like chairs and tables and cats and dogs and pens and ink and people. But as Charlie sat unravelling in his chair at his table, with his tupperware and his blueberries and his fragile earthy humanness, he realised for the first, and for the last time, there is a correlative claim, which haunts the first: there are certain items that, if we are to persist in our everyday affairs and to preserve any semblance of sanity, we must at all costs *ignore*. For should we acknowledge these items, should we find our conceptual framework so changed that we might pick them out in the world, we cannot help but invite them – all of them – to do the very same to us.

such brittle bodies

such brittle bodies II.xi.§13

we have II.xxi.§60

bodies I.iii.§17

possessed of II.xx.§7

vehement pain II.xxi.§39

that topping uneasiness II.xxi.§39

hunger, thirst, heat, cold, weariness II.xxi.§46

such grosser sensible bodies II.iv.§1

so II.xxi.§46

pitiful II.iii.§17

incomplete II.xvii.§15

broken I.ii.§11

so I.ii.§10

weak I.iii.§18

that some II.ii.§1

have thought themselves made of glass II.xi.§13

such brittle bodies II.xi.§13

. . .and the mind is I.i.§5

more I.i.§5

miserable I.iii.§5

by far I.i.§24

She ate her lunch in the lecture hall, slowly, a packet of crisps and a can of Coke followed by a half-melted chocolate bar. Not long after she had tucked the last, wispy strand of caramel into her mouth, the lecturer arrived, carrying a stack of handouts and looking harried. He seemed surprised to see Jay sitting there in the second row – but he smiled and said something cheerful, which she didn't quite catch. In a bid to look busy, she put the empty Coke can in the empty bag of crisps and walked to the front of the lecture hall where she put them both in the bin. Then she returned to her seat and pretended to read.

The book she was pretending to read was John Locke's *Essay Concerning Human Understanding*, which she had found for £3.50 in the second-hand section of the local bookshop where she often spent her lunch-breaks. It was a tatty copy, smudged, dog-eared, with a broken spine and a luminous rainbow of highlighted text that stretched between the pages. The highlighted words did not appear to be organised by any unifying logic and said things like:

"Dogs or Elephants do not think" II.i.§19

and

"The Caribes were wont to geld their children,

on purpose to fat and eat them." I.ii.§9

The words scurried in front of her, doing anything but be understood. The lecturer, meanwhile, began placing handouts on seats around the hall. He was a big man and when he reached the second row he avoided squeezing past her and instead handed her a sheaf, smiled and said something incomprehensible. She took the papers and nodded to show she had understood (which she hadn't). He smiled confusedly, then worked his way back towards the front of the room. He kept jangling what sounded like a set of keys in his trouser pockets, but could also have been coins.

On the bench in front of Jay, the book's highlighted text said:

"*'Tis impossible for the same thing to be, and not to be*" II.ii.§4

It was eleven o'clock and the other students began milling in. The seats started to fill up. It was a popular course and there were a lot of people, but for some reason no students sat on Jay's row. It wasn't a large lecture hall and very soon students were asking other students to "move along". Jay's stomach clenched. She sniffed, then awkwardly inspected the soles of her trainers. Nothing. Did she have something on her face? The camera on her phone told her she hadn't. Eventually, a pale girl in a leather jacket sat a few seats down and Jay experienced a disproportionate sense of relief. Two more students followed and she passed them handouts. Shortly afterwards, the lecture began.

The lecture was about John Locke's account of personal identity. Jay had done the assigned readings and some additional ones too. The lecturer, who was called Michael Flaherty, or Mike, stood at the whiteboard and explained that Locke's account of personal identity could be found in the second Book of the second edition of the *Essay Concerning Human Understanding*, which was, he said, less of an "essay" as people understood essays today and more of a "hefty tome". "Don't worry, I won't be asking you to write one of these!" he said. There was laughter. Mike scribbled notes on the board with a green marker pen. He explained that personal identity is grounded in continued consciousness and that continued consciousness is evidenced by experiential memory. He explained the "is of identity" by saying:

"Samuel Clemens is the same person as Mark Twain."

Jay doodled in the margins of the *Essay* which was not an essay. Mark Twain was the author of *Huckleberry Finn*, a book she had read when she was in secondary school and knew contained repeated usage of the n-word. Mike refrained from mentioning this. He also refrained from mentioning Locke's involvement in the Transatlantic Slave Trade and the disenfranchisement of Native Americans, which Jay had read about in the secondhand section of the local bookshop.

She flicked through her copy of the *Essay*. The highlighted text said:

"uneasiness or discomposure of the mind. . ." II.xx.§12

Finishing his introduction, Mike rubbed his head and clipped the lid back on his marker pen. He ran his fingers down the front of his shirt. This was the moment she dreaded. It was a moment in which she experienced a "discomposure of the mind". Mike looked around the room, then asked if there were any questions.

"Any questions?"

It was unreasonable, she thought, to feel this level of panic. There was no reason for these anxious contractions in her chest, or the sudden pockets of condensation where her palms touched the wooden bench in front of her. Apart from anything else, Mike was known for being generous with his students and even when they asked basic questions he would nod, considering them all with equal seriousness. He would answer in that breathy way of his and occasionally say "good point" and everyone would feel A-OK.

Today was the day, she told herself, to ask a question. She raised her hand. She had a question and it was, she thought, a good question. It was a much more relevant question than many of the questions already being asked, which were about exam dates and essay deadlines and course materials. She held her hand steady. Mike saw it, acknowledged it, and she lowered her arm. Unfortunately, a queue had formed and before she could ask her question Mike would have to work his way around the room. She began to regret her decision to raise her hand. What if someone asked her question before she had a chance? If that happened, she would have to shrug and say,

"Actually it's already been answered."

She could feel her throat tightening and noticed that the previous owner of her copy of the *Essay* had ringed the words:

"Foolish Maid" II.xxxiii.§10

Her heart began to vibrate in an unusual manner. To her right and left, hands were slowly lowering as the lecturer answered their questions and responded to their comments. If nobody asked her question, *she* would have to ask her question. But what if it wasn't a good question after all? Very soon, Mike would turn to her and so would everyone else and she would be forced by what Locke would call the corporate person of the student body to say something. She reassured herself that Mike would interpret her question generously. The girl in the leather jacket had just referred to the *Essay Concerning Human Understanding* as the *Enquiry Concerning Human Understanding*, which Jay knew was by David Hume rather than John Locke, and Mike was in the process of gently correcting her. If Jay made a similar mistake, Mike would gently correct her too. Jay knew from an article she had read the previous evening that David Hume believed Black people were inferior to white people, but this was not something Mike mentioned. There was only one student ahead of her in the queue and she had begun to sweat heavily. For some reason her body produced far more sweat than it needed to and apparently far more than anyone else's body.

The book said:

"Bodily torments" II.xxi.§60

The question before Jay's was short and quickly answered, though she had no idea what it was. Mike blinked, looked around the room, then nodded at her in that good-natured way of his and she heard herself begin to speak, slightly too loudly. She moderated the volume of her voice and asked whether or not Locke's views about race fed into his views about personal identity.

"Do Locke's views about race feed into his views about personal identity?"

Mike's friendly face sank in on itself, like a lemon left out in the sun. She paused and tried to pull her question back in, which meant her sentence finished with an abrupt slurping sound. Mike was blinking again and rubbing his head and she saw he was embarrassed. He was not embarrassed because he didn't know the answer, though he didn't know the answer – he was embarrassed for her, for Jay. He was embarrassed that she had asked such a strange question. He mumbled,

"That's not really . . ."

He didn't even give her a complete sentence before moving onto the next question, which she was unable to hear because of the sudden thudding in her ears. The session continued but the embarrassment thickened around her, mottling the air.

"shame" I.ii.§13

said the book,

"makes the heart sick" II.xxi.§32

It had been an irrelevant question. She had misunderstood the nature of the lecture, which was about metaphysics and not race. The girl in the leather jacket was glancing at her and Jay turned away too slowly to miss the look on her face. She was mouthing something that Jay was unable to understand. Jay stared at the page in front of her. The text, highlighted in pink, read simply:

"Fool" II.xx.§51

A young white man in glasses was asking a question now. His words lacked form and purpose, but Mike was nodding slowly and humming in agreement. It was the kind of noise an old sofa makes when you sit on it too heavily and the springs give way. Jay told herself to relax, but her thoughts sluiced unpleasantly over and under each other. For want of something to do with her hands, she started to turn the pages of the book. It said,

"Stop" II.xvii.§4

It said, " 'tis *uneasiness* alone" II.xxi.§36

"bear with this" Introductory letter

She experienced an odd queasiness in the pit of her stomach. The young man was still asking his question, "more of a comment" he was saying, and Mike was still nodding and humming and the other students had begun to join in. Heads were nodding and humming all around the room, but Jay's head was bowed as she stared fixedly at the pages of her book. The book said,

"attend to the motions of the mind" II.xxxii.§7

"consider the" II.ii.§3

"advancement of knowledge" I.i.§27

"There is no Body, I think, so senseless as to deny, that there is pleasure in knowledge" II.xxi.§43

The text was highlighted with a luminous yellow, a shade from a frequency of light that seemed to Jay to hover on the margins of the visual field. She focused on the phrase "there is pleasure in knowledge". Her fingers tripped along the paper's edge and when the pages settled again, the book said,

". . . good pleasure" II.xv.§12

"great pleasure" II.xxxiii.§15

She pressed a hand to her cheek. Warmth had been replaced with a coolness that had nothing to do with the lecture hall's erratic air conditioning. It was ridiculous, she told herself. It was her imagination. But when, a second later, she wondered what organised this seemingly random rainbow of notes, the pages fell again and said,

"Man" I.iv.§12

"*Man*" IV.v.§7

"a Man" II.xxvii.§8

"a very honest and pious Man" II.xxvii.§8

In the distance she could hear the young man with glasses talking and talking and Mike humming. They were standing at the board now, the young man drawing something with the marker pen, while the others had started to file out. The girl in the leather jacket had collected her books and was chatting to another girl in a hooded jacket. They kept glancing over at Jay, but she remained sitting and told herself that her book was a book, just a book, no matter how the pages fell. It said,

"Childish Peevishness" I.i.§5

It said,

"I am" I.i.§1

"a man" I.i.§1

A book, Jay repeated to herself.

"If so" I.i.§21

it said,

". . . a book not everyday to be met with" I.ii.§9

It occurred to Jay that she was entering a dangerous place. Mike and the young man were still talking at the front of the room, but she felt suddenly and very acutely concerned for her safety. She was moving alone through an unfamiliar space and found she could not stop moving, she could not turn back, but would have to press on. Her hands flicked through the pages of the book, almost automatically, and it said,

"pain" II.x.§

"agony" II.xxxii.§14

"despair" Introduction.§6

It said,

"No" II.i.§10

"it is quite remote from my Thoughts" II.xxii.§11

It was just a book, she told herself. She understood books. Books made sense to her in a way that people often didn't. This book was just a book, even if it made her feel disjointed, unhooked, even if she felt it in the small of her back and the back of her head. The pages crinkled under her fingers, her fingerprints smudging those of its previous owners. It was just a book, she thought.

"I deny that" I.i.§14

It said,

"please" II.xxvii.§18

"Allow me a place in your good thoughts" Introductory letter

"... this" II.xiii.§22

"be that which is called good" I.xx.§43

Jay stared at the text. It was densely packed on the page and in places quite poorly registered. It was printed in an archaic, serif font, interspersed with irregular capitals. Jay knew a close homonym of "serif" was "seraph", which she also knew was a type of angel. But the book was a book, she thought. The pages turned almost unbidden. It said:

"... It is true" II.i.§16

"I confess" II.iv.§5

"Still" Introductory letter

"I am" II.viii.§24

"A thinking intelligent Being" II.xxvii.§9

A book, thought Jay.

"I am" II.ix.§8

"a Miracle" II.x.§5

The spine rolled along her fingertips.

"I had a mind" II.xxvii.§8

it said,

"now" I.ii.§3

"quite lost" II.x.§5

"I am absent" Introductory letter

The young man with glasses was shaking Mike's hand. The lecturer hummed, then watched as this student slung a rucksack over his shoulders, adjusted his glasses and left. Mike, who seemed to have forgotten about Jay, began to pack up his things. There were handouts left around the room, but he made no effort to tidy them up because one of the domestic workers would do that later. On his way out, he noticed Jay still sitting there in the second row and mumbled something, which could have been Goodbye. There was no smile this time and he didn't wait for her to reply before taking the stairs two at a time and pushing his way through the swinging double doors. Jay stared at the book. The book said,

"*Illiterate*" I.iii.§27

"unintelligent, intractable *Changeling*"

It said,

"Blackmoor" I.i.§25

"all names for the same thing" II.xxviii.§11

"Savage" I.iii.§17

"savage"

She could put it in the bin, she thought. It had only cost £3.50 and she could read it online. The Gutenberg Archive was an excellent resource. That's what Mike had said. An excellent resource. She didn't need the book. She would put it in the bin with her Coke can and the wrapper from her chocolate bar and the empty packet of crisps.

"This I cannot forbear" Introductory letter

She pushed it away from her. The spine squeaked on the bench's polished surface. The pages fanned in front of her. The marked words shone, pink, blue, green and yellow. The book said,

"at the end" II.xiii.§21

"you are" II.xvii.§15

"nothing" II.xxviii.§11

It said,

"you are" Introductory letter

"Nihil" II.xxviii.§11

"a void space, beyond the utmost bounds of body" II.xvii.§4

"the absence of light" II.viii.§5

"you are"

"darkness" II.viii.§6

"Decay" II.ix.§14

"a carcass"

The book's binding feathered, exposing the threads that held its pages together. Jay had heard other students explain how much they loved the smell of old books, but old books smelled of lignin, an organic substrate found in rotting bark and wood, and of glue, which is made from the hooves and bones of dead horses. As the water-spotted pages turned, it was this smell that engulfed her. The book said,

"evil?" II.ix.§13

"It is. . ." II.ix.§14

"a weakness to which all men are so liable" II.xxxiii.§4

It said,

"now" Introductory letter

"submit to" I.i.§28

"me" I.ii.§4

"Now"

"submit" I.ii.§23

"your mind" II.xvii.§6

"your" Introductory letter

"body" II.xvii.§6

"J" I.ii.§2

"your" Introductory letter

"soul" II.xxvii.§9

"submit" I.i.§28

"to your" Introductory letter

"master" II.xi.§7

"child" II.xxxiii.§13

*

It lay there, half-open, on a bench in the lecture hall. It was an old book, dog-eared and tatty, its pages bent as though it had been flung on the desk or twisted in some miserable grip. But there was no one around to fling it. Someone, perhaps more than one person, had gone through it with a highlighter pen. Lurid greens, blues and pinks dotted and lined the yellowing pages. There was no obvious order or sense to them individually, but looking within that mess of paper from a particular angle, an interested reader might see words ringed in jagged ink.

Read from a certain view, the book said,

"I am" I.i.§1

"the most dangerous one" II.xxxiii.§18

It said,

"I am" I.iii.§6

"A Devil" II.xxvii.§8

"Doom" II.xxvii.§22

"I am" I.i.§1

"a God" I.iv.§11

"God" I.ii.§5

"GOD" IV.xx.§3

Empty Man III: Marcia (2010)

"...what can I get you? hmmm? ...no absolutely not... no put that away it's on me you're an impoverished student for god's sake... a doctoral student that's even worse haha... now what would you like ...a cappuccino? a latte? a hot chocolate? good great fantastic a latte I'll have a latte too... two lattes please we'll be sitting over there yes in the window-seat by the man with the– yes that's right the one with the hoodie... and excuse me ...excuse me... before you go could you stamp my card? ...my *card* ...yes... actually I think I'm entitled to *two* stamps... it's a stamp per *drink* not per *visit* thank you... thank you......my god did you see that *look*? haha you'd think I'd insulted his mother– ...and I hate being pedantic but I *am* entitled to two stamps... anyway hopefully he won't spit in our coffees would you like a glass of water it's nice they put a slice of cucumber in it... no? suit yourself haha I need to stay hydrated in this weather I'm sweating buckets... exactly... good... okay now we're all settled why don't you tell me what this is about hmmm? ...well yes... yes... I read it and goodness it sounds like you've been contending with an awful lot you've been through the wringer... poor you poor poor you... and that's why I thought it would be helpful if we had a little chat just you and me I want to know exactly what you're dealing with before we think about pursuing more formal lines of investigation... as much for your benefit as anyone else's because believe me these things can end up being dreadfully drawn-out I've had a lot of experience with these kinds of complaints and the emotional cost can be punishing– ...well yes I understand you might be feeling an urgency *now* but if you raise an official complaint it can take weeks if not months if not *years* to resolve– ... no of course that doesn't mean we shouldn't pursue it not at all... I'm just saying it's important to have the targets lined up before we take action– ...well because as far as I could tell there isn't actually much *evidence* to support your claims and the evidence you described is circumstantial and of course *I* believe you and it sounds dreadful really dreadful but the fact is unless you've got substantial evidence hard proof it's unlikely you'll get anywhere and that's just the depressing reality of it trust me I've experienced my fair share of this sort of thing you don't spend twenty years in academia without encountering a few haha *unsavoury* characters– ... well no yes no of course unsavoury isn't the right word but you know what I mean haha I'm trying to be polite... no of course I realise it's more than just *him* but that makes things even more difficult institutional complaints are almost never successful– ...ah here are our drinks– ... thank you... wonderful... could you put them just there and do you have any sugar? sugar I said sugar thank you yes... now haha whoops excuse the slurping where were we? ...that's right yes institutional complaints are almost never successful and legally well it's rather murky territory... oh it's *completely* valid and I understand the theory one hundred per cent but practically it's very difficult and I think we ought to consider *alternative* ways forward because once you send an official letter that's a completely different can of worms and things can get very messy and are you sure you want to get embroiled in all that?

with things as they are?...it might just be better to keep your head down...below the parapet as it were...because the truth of the matter is these old boys are all retiring anyway... the dinosaurs are dying out haha...and I know it's not quite as satisfying as forcing them out but maybe the best course of action in this situation is just to wait? ...no no no it's not that it's not *worthwhile* or *important* and of course they need to be held *accountable* but I'm thinking about *you* you see and I just wonder whether this is helpful for *you*...believe me I'm completely behind the sentiment and gosh I admire you for taking a stand because god knows I'm sick and tired of the way that lot act... the stories I could tell you would make your hair curl... if it weren't already so curly haha... but I have a responsibility to *you* and I don't want you getting caught up in a nasty situation... right... right... no I understand that it's already pretty nasty– ...well yes exactly... yes... oh that's reminded me would you like a pastry? maybe we could share one I saw they have cherry bakewells do you like cherry bakewells no? well I think I might get one... excuse me... excuse me... yes could we please have a bakewell a cherry bakewell with the two forks? thank you so very much... yes just bring it over... now where were we that's right I was saying I think you should finish your research I think you should keep your head down... for the time being at any rate... because honestly it's not worth trying to change anything *right now* you need to focus on your studies finish your phd and then you'll be in a much better place to raise these kinds of issue... once you're *part* of the institution... from the inside... otherwise you're going to exhaust yourself you're going to *burn out*... no no not at all I'm not saying *let it go* ...all I'm saying is why don't you leave it with me for the time being let me do a bit of digging and there might be better ways of approaching it– ... ah and here comes the bakewell ...thank you that looks delicious but I asked for two forks... *two*... yes that's right thank you... and could I get another stamp please? ...I beg your pardon what do you mean stamps are only for drinks why would they only be for drinks that's completely ridiculous I'm spending just as much money on cakes if not more– . . . I don't want to get into an argument about this but I'm a regular customer here and no one's ever mentioned this nonsense before . . .no of course I'm not saying you're lying I just think it's a ludicrous policy. . . yes. . . okay. . . no nothing else for the time being. . . thank you. . . gosh. . . what a petty little man haha normally they're very nice here the manager knows me you see. . . anyway yes I think the best thing for you to do is leave it with me for now. . . you didn't send that email to anyone else did you? no? good that's good that means we can have a think and I'll investigate if that sounds okay? you know I'm really glad you came to talk to me before you did anything haha more dramatic– . . .my goodness this cake is incredibly stale. . . do you think our friend over there did that on purpose gave us a stale cake? what a petty man. . . sorry I'm getting distracted but goodness me it's like cardboard. . . anyway. . . anyway I was actually going to contact you about something else as well completely unrelated did you hear about that research post over in– . . .yes in the states exactly that's the one. . . I know. . . it's with. . . yes and she's brilliant and I was thinking that your work on– . . .exactly you'd be a *perfect* fit for this and of course I know the research director there she's a good friend of mine from my oxford days and I was wondering whether you'd considered applying because you certainly should and if you needed a reference I'd be *very* happy to help it's really the least I could do given what an *asset* you are to the department . . .no you *are* honestly– . . .god this bakewell. . . it tastes like sandpaper how do they get away with selling this stuff? anyway why don't you write up a rough research proposal and I'll get in touch with Diane. . . great. . . and you'll leave this email business with me and I'll have a think about how best to proceed. . . yes? I'm so glad you came to talk to me about all this it's a really desperate situation but we'll get you through it don't worry and hopefully without too much bother and in the meantime you press on with your studies and we'll get you this postdoc... and now I suppose I should go and see this man about this bakewell haha... no of course not... I told you I'm paying ...you can get the next one haha ..."

The Locked Room

The room existed halfway between the third and fourth floor of 17 Mordell Square. "Room", perhaps, is too grand a word. It was little more than a glorified cupboard, a walk-in closet just large enough for a small grey desk and those nasty little stools one sees standing unused in the corners of assembly halls. The walls were a thoughtless white, scuffed and dirty from decades of jostling bodies, and lined with neither bookcases, nor bookshelves, nor books. If these walls could talk, they would say *nothing*, they displayed *nothing*, save for the grubby ghosts of Blu Tack where an office calendar had once hung.

Still, at least the room was bright, unlike the dank, windowless chambers in the basement of the department. It possessed a sash window of medium size, painted shut and singly glazed. A draught wound its way through the cracks in the pane, and outside in the Square the tree-branches cut the sky into a spray of shattered glass. On the mantel above a small bricked-in fireplace, a forgotten clock had stopped ticking at three o'clock precisely.

It was an inconsequential room, a room easily missed on the journey downstairs from the seminar rooms to the graduate kitchenette. In recent years it had received few visitors, all unhuman: woodlice, spiders, a fat and dusty bluebottle that was even now doing the rounds overhead. The bluebottle hovered by a lonely lightbulb embedded in an excessively ornate ceiling rose. It produced the kind of atonal buzzing that would have driven researchers to distraction and worse, a buzzing that modulated the hum from the radiators, generating a sound that registered only at the subdural level, beyond hearing but sufficiently present to make those exposed to it faintly nauseous. This was the only material impact of the radiators, which, while scaldingly hot to the touch, did very little to warm the dead air of this resolutely inconsequential room.

The fly buzzed. Dust motes fell from cornices, paint peeled. And then, *unusually*, the door handle, made of twisted brass, began grudgingly to turn. The bluebottle settled on the ceiling-rose and rubbed the turquoise of its compound eyes. It twitched this way and that. The handle rattled metal bones. The key, if ever there had been one, was well and truly lost, and with a gulp of stale air the door swung open. A tangle of students fell in.

There were four. Hannah, Niall, Sam and Alex. Masters students, they were clearly comfortable in the departmental hierarchy, but lacking so far the dead-eyed stare of the long-term researcher. They gasped for breath. Hannah, tall, athletically built, strode inside and thumped her stack of books on the table, sending puffs of dust into the room. Sam and Niall followed her. Alex lingered by the door.

"Are you sure we're allowed in here?"

Hannah rolled her eyes.

"It was open, wasn't it?"

Yes, somehow it had been open, though Alex had never tried the door before, had never even seen it. She entered, despite an instinctive timidity, as Sam and Niall piled their rucksacks in the corner. Sam, beautiful Sam, dropped onto a dusty stool and pulled out her phone.

"Did anyone see Sadie downstairs?"

Alex shook her head. Niall shrugged. Hannah's eyebrows rose.

"You invited *Sadie*?"

It was clear from the vertical furrow that now subdivided Hannah's forehead that she did not particularly approve of Sadie. Sam ignored her and turned her attention to Alex who was hovering nervously by the window.

"Are you going to sit down or what?"

Or what? Chastened, Alex readjusted her glasses and took a seat by the bricked-up fireplace. Three o'clock, the mantelpiece clock still said. She let her coat shuffle from her shoulders, a shed skin, and wondered why, exactly, she'd let Sam and the others persuade her to join them. It wasn't as if they wanted her there. She was inessential. She wasn't even taking Metaphysics, she should be writing her essay on the Pre-Socratics. Glumly, she watched as Hannah squared the corners of her book stack. Outside, lorries ground their way around the Square – and overhead, the bluebottle sat, silent, motionless, unblinking with its thousand eyes.

"*Alex.*"

". . . I'm sorry?"

Hannah was looking at her with an expression of more than mild irritation – but whatever she'd asked, Alex hadn't heard it. Niall was smirking, either to himself or Sam. Alex felt her cheeks grow hot.

". . . I'm not actually doing metaphysics," she said, quietly, and wished, not for the first time, that she had a less tremulous voice. Sam said (and Alex believed her) that if you sounded apologetic it made everyone think you had something to apologise for. Sam never apologised. Hannah scowled and extracted a sheaf of neatly stapled papers from her bag, pushing them towards the others.

"I guess this means *I'm* doing the intro?"

"I guess so," muttered Sam, whose attention had returned to her phone.

Alex glanced at her watch, which like the clock on the mantelpiece said three o'clock. She shouldn't have come with them. The deadline for her essay was tomorrow. She should leave. Could she leave? She glanced towards the door, annoyed at herself for sitting so far away. From outside came the enthusiastic rumbling of undergraduates charging up and down the stairs. She stared longingly at the door handle.

The door handle began to turn.

For the second time that day, that week, that year, for the second time in as many decades, that snarled brass teardrop began to shake. Once. Twice. Three times. Then it jerked upwards abruptly, then down, a peculiar spasmodic movement, and the next second a young woman with a shaved head fell into the room.

"Sadie!" Sam leapt from her chair and reached over Niall to give the newcomer a hug. Alex watched and tried to smile. Sam had never hugged *her* like that, not that she had any reason to. Niall joined in and was quickly caught up in the snarl of arms and earrings. Alex found herself moved to look elsewhere. She leaned back in her chair and stared at the ceiling, where she found a bluebottle staring back at her, polishing its multifaceted eyes in an almost perverted fashion.

"I know I'm late," Sadie was saying. "I've been up and down like a thousand times. God, I'm so *sweaty*. I could have sworn you said the basement-"

"*Anyway.*"

Hannah placed her hands palm-down on the tabletop. There was an edge to her voice, thought Alex, sharp like the furrow in her forehead.

"We were actually just getting started . . ."

The others appeared not to have heard her. Sadie removed her jacket and flung it onto the pile of bags. Squeezing past Alex, she perched on the windowsill. Alex tucked herself into the table, feeling the line of laminated wood press across her stomach. Sadie's elbow brushed the back of her head and Alex lowered her gaze and saw a collection of paint scabs on her sleeve. She brushed at them furtively until they crumbled into the fabric of her jumper, becoming a gritty white smear.

"We need to get started," Hannah was saying. "The exam's next week."

"Hannah," Sam's eyes flashed. "*Chill out.*"

"Yeah, Hannah, *chill out*", repeated Sadie.

Alex stared at the ceiling, listening to them bicker, their voices rising and falling, running fast then slow, intermingling with the clank of the pipes, the tapping of the walls. She pulled a length of thread from the hem of her jumper and idly began wrapping it around her forefinger. Round and round and round. She shouldn't be here, she told herself, and watched the skin grow taut and red, pulsing, then mottled. Pain, and she loosened her grip. She unwound the thread and inspected the glowing white grooves it had left on her skin. Beside her, Sadie slipped from the windowsill and perched on the corner of the table. Her hands moved delicately around her throat as she spoke. All this perching seemed unnecessary, since there was a perfectly good stool to sit on.

On the other side of the table, Hannah had pulled a handful of highlighters from her rucksack and had begun working her way pointedly through the text while the others chatted. Quick, angry movements. Lines of luminous green and yellow criss-crossed the paper. Every so often, Hannah would glance at Sadie and the furrow on her forehead would deepen.

Everything is water.

The thought occurred to Alex out of nowhere. Everything is water, everything is liquid, flowing and fluid. She turned to stare out of the window and saw the planes trees rustle in the wind. She was water. Hannah was water too. Siphoned, channelled, directed and dammed. They moved where they were told to move, flowed where they were told to flow. Everything was water. Was it Thales who said that, or Heraclitus? She would have to check. She could write about it in her essay. On the other side of the table, Niall laughed at Sadie's impression of Professor Grover and behind them the radiators began to shudder and shake with what seemed like fellow feeling. Laughter, bubbling up from the boiler room. Outside, the sun slipped anaemic over the horizon and the plane trees shivered with the cold.

Within the radiators, rust-flecked water span in darkness. It ran against their ragged metal innards, now hot, now cold, now streaming past the clusters of knotted cilia that had formed over the years from calcium sediment. It had been decades since they'd been bled, but every now and then a minor fissure would release a gasp of foetid air and an evil hiss into the room. They gurgled as ancient water churned within them. Alex listened and picked at a swatch of yellowed sellotape on the tabletop. She imagined she heard a distant voice, thin and wheedling in the walls of this inconsequential room. *Everything is water.*

Above, on the wedding-cake cornicing, the bluebottle continued to rub its eyes. Was it crying, Alex wondered. Did flies cry? She had an odd impression that like everything else in the room the bluebottle was waiting for her to leave. *Her*, but no one else. She should leave. She returned its gaze and imagined its tiny hairs bristling in recognition. Its horrible, trumpet-like proboscis sucked vainly at the air. How old was it? Immemorial. Thick, round, a dirty clot stuck to the ceiling. Did flies die of natural causes? What a funny thing to think, she thought.

As she watched, the insect was shaken by a minuscule spasm, a bodily tremor that shivered out to the tips of its wings. It dropped, then flew, describing clear, perfectly angled geometries. The next moment it was sitting on the windowsill beside Alex, stroking its legs in anticipation. The white walls whispered. The radiators churned. *Leave*, they told her.

She had an essay to write. This was the thought now pumping back and forth in her mottled brain, slipping against the cavity of her skull, rusty red-flecked and alkaline. Everything was water.

Alex was water. On her surface this single thought floated, scum caught in the whorls and eddies on the wake. It was a thin sheen of thought that flowed but played no role in the movement of her body. But *something* had caught, something on the surface had snagged. Her arm dropped and picked her jacket from the floor. Was she doing this? The thought was hers, but Alex had the impression some deeper current was pulling her forward. It was a familiar feeling, to be directed. She folded her jacket and stood up. She wanted to leave and she was leaving. The fly buzzed by her head, that undulating drone interweaving with the pops and hisses of the radiator, the whispers from the walls. She was leaving.

Hannah rolled her eyes. "Brilliant. Now Alex is going."

Sadie and Sam glanced over and waved unenthusiastically. Niall smiled an empty smile. Alex shuffled past them to the door. She was alone, it seemed, in feeling the growing pressure in the room, the build-up of rotten air, thoughts needing to be bled. Her fingers found the brass handle, unusually cool – and for all the twisted metalwork, it was smooth, pliant, almost flesh-like. She turned it. Once. Twice. Three times. Its metal bones clicked and then, there, it was open and she was walking through and free.

On the other side, an unexpected key extruded from the keyhole.

Whatever current was carrying her pulled the door closed again. She caught a final glimpse of Niall, sighing, Hannah stacking papers, Sam and Sadie deep in conversation. Everything was water, and with the smoothness and subtlety of water, and the radiators still throbbing and the fly still buzzing in her ear, Alex slowly locked the door then pocketed the key.

She descended the stairs. Outside, she stood on the curb of 17 Mordell Square and watched the last rays of a sinking sun disappear behind the treetops. Everything was water, she told herself. Everything was fluid, fluctuating spirals in a constant flux of change. High up behind her, in that inconsequential room, now locked and sealed and airless, halfway between the third and fourth floor, in that nowhere space rarely found, the bluebottle buzzed, the radiators hissed, the white walls whispered, and down here Alex waited, and waited, for someone to tell her what to do.

Campus Rumpus I–IV

Campus Rumpus I

The Socratic Quarterly (April) vol. 12 no. 5

In the first instalment of his new column Professor Benedict March takes us for a turn around the college grounds and introduces us to the joys of cloistered life.

Consider the doors. Ancient oak and heavy-set. Lacquered with a varnish of bombazine black that seems to suck the light from the very air. And closed. Wholeheartedly closed to all save a select and secret few. Mervyn's is a Fellows College. There are no students here and, Russell forbid, certainly no *tourists*. There is a small hatch through which the porter can turn you away. But not today. Today, I shall be your guide, the Virgil to your hapless Dante—and like those luckless Latins we must pass first through hell to get to heaven. The Porter's Lodge.

The Porter's Lodge is where our porter—whom, for the sake of anonymity, I shall call *O'Malley*—is lodged. A hessian-sack of a man, he is filled to the gills with potatoes and unpleasantly abrasive. It is a daily chore to walk through the Lodge and suffer his malingering looks and incomprehensible mutterings. If porters could talk, I daresay we would not understand them, and I rarely deign to try. Some of our Fellows regard him as "an Institution". I suppose he shares passing similarities to some, but only sewage works and knacker's yards. Foul-smelling but necessary.

Having navigated the labyrinth of pigeonholes and mawkish college notices, having evaded O'Malley's unwanted ministrations, one finds oneself emerging here, into the verdant idyll of the First Quadrangle. The City bells are singing in the distance – but you will notice that Mervyn's own bell is silent, its clapper wrapped in linen following the complaints of "excessive clanging" from our current Provost. We are a quiet College. Free of crunchy gravel, our paths are lined with worn-down paving slabs. Slippers are encouraged. Though it is less than a hundred metres away, the sounds from the high street are muffled and dreamlike. Were one to stand in the centre of the Quad and close one's eyes, it would be easy to believe, as Berkeley did, that the outside world has ceased to exist.

Let us continue. Single-file, please. We shall take the western path around the Sod, beneath the crawling ivy and busts of long-dead benefactors. Whatever occurs, please do not walk upon the grass. The last person to do so (Woolf) became a lesbian. Regard instead the walls. Sandstone from the fourteenth century, a sedimentary shortbread of a brick that has weathered the ravages of time surprisingly well. Every so often you will see a piece of graffito scratched into the stone commemorating the College's not unimpressive history of oarsmanship: "Head of the River 1643" reads one. "Lent Bumps 1818" reads another. A third is a picture of what appears to be a long leaking nose with two enflamed nostrils.

Walking towards us from the south end of the Quad you will see a groundskeeper, whom I imagine is called William. Every college has a William of some description. Ours is an hale and hearty lad of fifty-odd who insists on wearing shorts and a tool-belt, and is as thick as the two short planks he is forever carrying across his shoulder. Greet him if you like—his dialect is soothing. Like O'Malley, he is considered "an institution" (though n.b. the lower-case 'i'). I suppose he is not unlike the postal service: relatively dependable, though all too often tardy.

We may pause for a moment, by the entrance to the Senior Library. There is a bench here, polished by a hundred years of worsted buttocks. Take a seat. On the other side of the Quadrangle, beneath William's prize wisteria, you will see our Vice-Provost in his morning's repose, pipe cupped in hand, cup piping hot with the exotic herbal teas he favours. For the sake of our current arrangement, I will refer to him as Professor Crotchett.

Professor Crotchett has held his office for as long as anyone can remember. He is referred to as "a true Renaissance Man", so he cannot be far shy of five hundred. In Aristotle's great hierarchy of being, I believe his soul is now more vegetative than animal, and like the wisteria that blossoms overhead, the contributions he makes to College life are, I'm afraid, merely aesthetic. It is an issue that has been raised with the Provost and the Bursar, but these political men clearly value what others do not. They have nothing to fear from the Vice-Provost, because unlike the wisteria, dear Crotchett is not a climber.

Now, if you peer a little to the left of Crotchett you will see an iron gateway leading to a small sheltered square. A yew tree slumps hairily in the corner, red berries gleaming. At the conclusion to our first foray into campus life, it serves us well to note that one may exit Mervyn's in one of two ways: either via those jet-black doors beside the Porter's Lodge, or through here, the College's small but well-stocked graveyard, known affectionately as "The Scholar's Escape". It is in this sheltered corner, when Crotchett's time finally arrives, that the Renaissance

Man will be buried alongside his forebears and friends, in the warm, welcoming humus.

This, I think, is enough for our first sojourn. It is time for tea.

Mervyn College

Campus Rumpus II

The Socratic Quarterly (July) vol. 12 no. 6

It is Summer in Mervyn College and our College man and confidante, Benedict March, introduces us to the personages of the Second Quadrangle.

Summer is the only season in which the Fellows are permitted to walk across the sacred Sod of the Second Quad. On the very fairest days in the summer months, after lengthy consultation with the groundskeeper, and the signing of certain affidavits, the ceremonial hoops are erected, the mallets dusted off, and the College's champions take to the field to engage in the high drama of that most vigorous of gentlemanly sports: Croquet.

Walking through the tertiary atrium into the Quad, we find the audience piping vigorously in the shade of an overhanging elm. There, beside them, an array of cheese and cucumber sandwiches. The pseudonymous "Master Alberts" is up—which is to say, down, crouching in bleached white slacks, conducting the necessary calculations for his next shot. The geometry of croquet is a fine and subtle art. He stands, stretches his *tensor fascia lata*, then plays a blinder of an anti-duffer, sending the spectators into a lather of smoke and admiring murmurs.

If the groundskeeper is given advance notice, he will provide you with a deckchair. I recommend placing it here, by the Quad's eastern edge. This will give you an enviable view of both the croquet and one of the most precious jewels of the College's crown: The Press. Dating from the early sixteenth century, the Press is an impressive sandstone building, crawling with a veritable menagerie of comic gargoyles. Most of these figurines are brandishing quills or ink-blocks, some of them provocatively. The graffito carved into the doorjamb, by some early modern troublemaker, reads: *Lorem Ipsum.*

Mervyn's is the only college to possess its own working printing press. All our notices and unofficial documents—as well as our newspaper, *The Chap's Book*—are produced here by a team of ink-stained labourers under the direction of a functional if dull man whom I fancy to call "Claxton". Mr Claxton has the character of the woodcuts over which he so regularly enthuses. *Id est,* he is a blockhead. However, he is also a vast improvement on his predecessor, "Mr Brakebill", a fiery-haired Northerner who entertained certain peculiar ideas about typographical progress.

Allow me to explain: as you will doubtless be aware, each college possesses its own distinctive "style-sheet" and Mervyn's is no different. Here, one uses "one" far more than "you", and never uses "thou" except with dons or lovers. The details of footnoting and endnoting are too vulgar to mention here, and the em-dash—or em-rule—is considered prince among parentheses; commas are common, and en-rules, buttressed by spaces, are heresy. Mr Brakebill took it upon himself to "modernise" these age-old strictures—and thusly, towards his end he duly dashed. The barrage of complaints led to a heart-attack and his expulsion from College (in that order). We returned to our original rules.

Omnia cum Moore, as they say, *Ahem.*

Fortunately, Mr Claxton has none of Brakebill's radical ideas (one wonders if he has ideas at all), but is highly adept at multiplying texts. Recently, for example, he produced one hundred well-registered copies of Professor Crotchett's funerary notice, with need for neither *addenda* nor *errata*. At my request, he even managed to insert a tasteful memorial *fleuron* beside Crotchett's Christian name, a reference to the wisteria he so dearly loved.

Now, to return to the Second Quad. Sitting in one's deckchair, turning to the north, you will see an ivy-framed window with diagonal muntins. Look closely and you can see a figure standing at this window. He appears to be watching the croquet, but is almost certainly watching *you*. This is the College Bursar, a man we will call Professor Archibald Gleam. Professor Gleam is a suspicious man, who takes even his tea with a pinch of salt. He is the kind of man who *peers*. He is the kind of man who might call for an inquest following the death of a Vice-Provost. He is the kind of man who might wonder how exactly those yew berries found their way into said Fellow's cup. He is a penny-pincher of both money and facts, counting each out with a ruthless, bean-counting efficiency. Needless to say, he is the kind of man to whom other men are not kindly disposed.

By contrast, consider the Provost. Gleam's direct superior—and, following a recent promotion, my own. Professor "Norris" (shall we say) is commendably drab, with patches in all the right places. He is red-faced, white-faced, and blessed with a shock of silver hair on an almost perfectly spheroid head. With respect to the man's mind, he is an ant. Brains, however, have always been inessential to political flourishing and what Norris lacks in intellect he more than makes up for in rambunctiousness. Few would deny he is a jolly fellow, and the Fellows are fond of jollity. He is a summery man, and a summary of sorts for all that is pleasant about Mervyn's in these months. His is the voice of the college, loosing a great bellowing HURRAH when Master Alberts delivers his signature Dolly Rush and wins the game. Well done, Master Alberts!

Mervyn College

Campus Rumpus III

The Socratic Quarterly (October) vol. 12 no. 7

In this episode, we join our indefatigable College Man for "Formal Hall" and enjoy a smorgasbord of juicy anecdata from the history of Mervyn College.

The Dining Room, which overlooks the Third Quadrangle, is perhaps the most impressive of the College halls. It has a grand, vaulted ceiling carved with any number of mythical beasts, among them centaurs (rendered in the likeness of college forefathers) and women. There is a fine stone arch that reaches capaciously across the dais, and on the dais itself stands the High Table, where your guide daily takes his station.

Regard as well, the generously sized portraits that deck the wood-panelled walls. There is our founder, Edward VI, with all his fragile boyish charm. There is our ageing monarch, may Russell bless her and keep her, doing her very best to appear uncongested. Above them, and above the paintings of notable alumni, runs a frieze in bas-relief, which features the giggling serpents of Meryvn's crest. Higher still, we find a series of slender windows, a clerestory, against which branches rattle hoping, like many a precocious schoolboy, to gain entrance. The apertures admit little light. Illumination comes from the forest of candelabrae that run along the dining tables. Charming I'm sure, but a perennial hazard for Fellows' beards.

Few of my readers will have attended Formal Hall (though not, I suspect, for want of trying). Mervyn's is unique among the colleges in having Formal all year through and I'm pleased to say the quality of food is marginally above average. This evening, for instance, we start with an Oxford blue, celeriac soup, cured ham and "croutons" (small toast). The wine is French but otherwise passable.

Dinner is only brought out after Grace is given, *in nómine Russell et Spíritus Moore*. It is the Provost's delight to be served first, followed by the other members of the High Table and thence the Commons. The High Table is set with place-names and menus on white cards with gold trimming. They are fetching but superfluous, since everyone knows the order of seating and matters of courses as a matter of course. As the new Bursar, for instance, I am sat to the right of the new Provost, Archibald Gleam. I am entitled to an extra knob of butter with my bread. Our new Vice-Provost – let us call him Florian – sits facing me.

Professor Florian is an Aesthetician. He wears cravats and smirks excessively. Like all Aestheticians, he is unbearably, unconscionably *vain*. This evening, he is explaining, to nobody's interest, his latest publication – a monograph with the irritatingly floral title: *Jude The Ontologically Unsound: Degrees of Reality Among Hardy's Lesser Appreciated Personages*. I fancy he fancies it funny. Even the appearance of a Poached Hampshire trout does nothing to stem his burbling. Nor does Provost Gleam exert his right to stop what the statutes call "unedifying chatter". We are forced to listen to this coxcomb describe his "hierarchies of fictional being". We are told that Tess of the D'Urberville's is more metaphysically robust than the ghosts of "The Dead Quire", but less so than the County of Wessex. We are told that a truth embedded in fiction is a form of "transubstantiation". *Vanitas vanitatum, Omnia vanitas*. Were I Provost, such inanities would not be suffered.

Dessert is a foreign dish. A substance called "labneh" accompanies the rhubarb tart. It is "fine", though I would have preferred custard or curd. Suspicious as ever (more so, in light of recent events), Gleam waits and watches while others involve themselves. Once satisfied, he takes a bird-like bite and smiles a bird-like smile (a pointed one). Florian continues prattling.

Eventually, the servers emerge to collect the runcible cutleries and porcelain. They are silent people. Conversation with, and amongst, the kitchen staff is discouraged and in any case, few of them speak comprehensible English. The girls are some form of Eastern European, blonde-haired and blue-eyed, almost interchangeable in their waitress whites. Occasionally they are disciplined for wearing non-regulation ornaments. Uniforms must be kept uniform even when uncomfortable (I myself must suffer the scratchy ermine of my office). Alongside their frequent sartorial indiscretions these serving-girls are dishonest. I know, for instance, that they are easily swayed by issues of blackmail.

The Formal concludes as it always does, with brandy and cigars for the High Table—and for the commoners, the door. You may be interested to consider the Provost's Chalice, a much envied luxury of his post. It stands taller than the other glasses and sports, as well as the college crest, a fine gold-leaf lip. It is easily identifiable, even to the most short-sighted of serving-girls. Observe it now, in the flickering flames of the High Table's candles—multifaceted, crystalline. It refracts the light such that the brandy itself takes on a special and singular hue.

Raising it high, the Provost toasts to Queen and Mervyn, then sips it, and sips some more. Watch his Adam's apple bob. I do hope he doesn't choke.

Mervyn College

Campus Rumpus IV

The Socratic Quarterly (January) vol. 12 no. 8

In the final instalment of his column, the inimitable Benedict March considers the juridical processes of Mervyn College and by way of a parting gift, reveals one of the Provost's long-standing secrets.

[Readers will be pleased to discover that the full "Campus Rumpus" series is to be printed as a stand-alone supplement, forthcoming with April's issue. For more information please consult the Institute's Secretary.]

Outsiders to Mervyn's may be interested to learn that the College commands its own constabulary. Unlike the other Colleges, who have bowed to public pressure and disbanded their officers, Meryvn's is still governed by the Proctor and his "Bulldogs". The latter are justly named, since neither bulls nor dogs are known for their intelligence, but are bred instead for fealty. Their ruddy jowls and bowler hats make them easily recognisable (the men, not the dogs), and they can be relied upon to keep the peace in dining rooms and examination halls alike. Many carry a truncheon, a wooden staff known as a "Ruler".

There are, by tradition, two sites within the College grounds that the Bulldogs cannot enter.

The first is the Chapel, which abuts the Cemetery and the Second Quad. It is consecrated ground and as such extra-social. On entering the Chapel, you will note the mildew smell, the damp, the unpleasant coolness of the air. It is an atmosphere more amenable to the bodies lying in state than the bodies charged to watch them. Thus, even here, Professor Gleam found himself at my advantage and I admit I thought him a very smug corpse.

Around the chapel, you will see figures standing nonchalantly on small pedestals. There is Moore, there is Russell, there is Whitehead— as statuesque as you have ever seen them. By a large stone slab on the western wall, someone has carved the legend: *Praise be to Gödel.* The recently ex-Proctor was interred behind such a slab. At his funeral, two weeks prior, some commented that his death, like the man himself, was suspicious. The Bulldogs were called, but Bulldogs have a famously poor sense of smell and are unlearned in the pharmaceutical arts, so nothing was found.

Bulldogs are also unable to climb ladders. It is a ladder, hidden behind a delicately weighted and concealed panel in my new chambers, which leads to the *second* site that lies beyond the Proctor's jurisdiction.

"Bartleby's Folly" is a building specifically designed to look like a folly, or fake building, replete with *quadratura* and other architectural illusions. It was erected over a century ago to mark the passing of a famous (and generous) alumnus, whose mummified body remains interred somewhere in the rafters. From the east, the Folly takes on the aspect of a dome, from the west, a square tower—and from all the points of the compass it appears to be nothing more than a whimsy, a "Ha-Ha". Bartleby's Folly, however, is the hidden quarter of the Provost's Lodge.

If you look closely from the outside, you will see a small roundel in the north of the round-square *cupola*, in which a stained-glass window is set. From inside, this blue-green window offers an unprecedented view of the Third and Fourth Quadrangle and the buildings that adjoin them: the Senior Common Room, the Senior Library and the linen-stuffed clock-tower. On a Winter's day like today, with the snow falling thickly and the Fellows tucked in their beds with their pipes and their glasses of milk, one can chart College activities by following the footprints on the snow-laden sods. From this height, the lawns read like the pages of a book. Here we see the plodding of Bulldogs, there the doddering thoughts of the Proctor and Bedel. This way and that they wander. Untidy scrawl. They are searching, no doubt, for their new Provost, who regards them from the tranquillity of his tower.

The Provost remarks to himself that the odious Professor Florian was right: a fiction, a fake building, be it dome, tower or barn, is the perfect place to keep one's council. A folly is a wonderful place to hide.

Below, the footprints of these hapless Fellows form a confusion across the lawns. Worry not: the snow will melt and the confusion will disappear. Winter will roll back, another academic year will roll on, and the College will thrum again with the pleasant rhythm of our William's lawnmower. The wisteria shall bloom. The necessary pruning has occurred. The Provost's chalice shall be raised to good cheer. It was ever thus in Mervyn College, it ever is, and I say, here at the close, from the safety of my whimsy: it shall be forever more.

Mervyn College

The Master's Delight

Their heels sank into a plush cream carpet. Behind them the doors brushed closed, the sounds from the street grew muffled. A small, stout man with a pair of mutton-chops approached them, clasping his hands together,

"A very good evening to you, ladies. Do you have a reservation?"

"I'm a member," said Marcia, briskly.

The steward beamed through his mutton-chops . "You must have been one of our first! Are you here for a private function?"

"We are. Dinner in the Library."

"Do you know–"

"I do indeed. Upstairs and to the left."

"Enjoy your evening, madam."

"We most certainly shall."

Marcia led Grace towards the Ladies Cloakroom.

"One of their first what?" asked Grace.

"Women," Marcia replied, dryly.

Behind them, in the Dining Hall, the diners laughed and waiters danced their silent dances. Silverware shimmered and outside, the moon shimmered too, gibbous and lonely in the cold.

*

"It's horrific, isn't it?"

Shorn of their jackets and gloves, they entered the Library. Guests spun champagne flutes between fingers, music played. A row of attendants stood before the bookshelves, dispensing sparkling alcohol. Grace's eyes widened.

"I didn't think they'd have actual *servants*," she whispered. She stared at the long table arranged in front of them. "And why the fuck is there so much cutlery?"

"I did warn you."

"*Darling!*" The cry came from Marcia's left. "You're fashionably late!"

The Beautiful Hélène had detached herself from a gaggle of guests and was wafting towards them. Clasping Marcia by the shoulders, she deposited two well-formed kisses on either cheek. Turning, her eyes twinkled.

"And you must be Grace. By nature as by name, I see. What delicious hair you have."

"Thank you... Your hair is very nice too."

Hélène flicked it dismissively. "I *dye* it."

Before Grace could comment, a silver bell was rung and another steward – shaved this time, but still very ruddy – emerged to encourage the diners to take their seats. The doors to the Library were then closed and a pink ribbon was tied around the handles. The night drew the Club into its murky presence.

*

"I must say, your protégé is really rather delightful ..."

Gilroy's breath, Marcia noted, was already stale with sherry.

"... so eloquent," he enthused, "and not at all unlovely."

Marcia sighed, but silently. On the other side of the table, Philip had begun to pat Grace's hand, a surreptitious little gesture. Marcia watched her student move out of reach to adjust a hair fastener. These, she thought, were the strategies by which they were forced to navigate the world. Catching her student's eye she mouthed the words: *I'm sorry.* The girl's lip quirked upwards. Not for the first time, Marcia was struck by how confident she was. Though young. Too young, perhaps, for the Master's Dinner. Henry tapped his wine glass.

"Ladies and gentlemen." He coughed. "A moment's reflection if you please. Let us give thanks to the Master and to the Society for providing this evening's victuals . . ."

Marcia's gaze drifted. The room seemed not to have changed since her last visit – doubtlessly the result of continuous dusting and polishing by the Club's various charwomen. The upholstered sofas, the reading desks, the lamps. They were replacements – the originals having been destroyed during the war – but in many ways they were not replacements at all, just as the words of Henry's litany were new words but also the same words he recited every year.

". . . Maestrum Dominum Nostrum," she murmured with the others. On the other side of the table, Grace was trying to keep a straight face.

*

The starters were quickly dispensed with. The first course – of five – was wheeled out to approving murmurs. As always, the Beautiful Hélène had spent a considerable amount of time in conversation with the Club's kitchen creating an obscenely extravagant menu. Marcia glanced at the card on the silver stand in front of her.

Goose Liver, Spiced Port and Pear
Oxtail Consommé, Sweetbreads and Paillette D'Or
Braised Turbot, Sea Fennel and Shellfish Jus
Fillet of Beef, Smoked Bone Marrow, Celeriac
Master's Delight

Grand Cru Chocolate Mousse and Grue with Hazelnut
Coffee and Tea with Frivolities

Her heart flickered. Three seats down, Teddy was beginning what was likely to be a series of exponentially tedious speeches. Philip was explaining to Grace how to use a fish knife. Grace regarded him with cool disapproval. If anyone was to be deboned, Marcia thought, it was likely to be Philip. She corrected herself, given the circumstances. She was at the Club, after all.

A waiter appeared on her left and poured a thin braid of Grenache Blanc into a waiting wine glass. Her face already felt hot. Beside her, Gilroy dandled his glass in the crook of a hand.

"Beautiful bouquet," he sniffed, staring at Grace, "Full-bodied too."

Marcia frowned as Philip's bloodless hands crawled back towards her student. She took another sip of wine and felt a wave of giddiness wash over her. She really should eat something. On her plate, flakes of white flesh broke free from the intricate bone-work. Grace excused herself to go to the cloakroom – and for a moment, Marcia was gripped by a desperate hope that she would not ever come back.

*

Waiters bustled around the table, collecting bone china and cutlery. One of them, a redheaded man with fragile fingers, stood uncertainly at Grace's shoulder (she had returned from the cloakroom). He asked,

"Has madam finished?"

"Oh yes, thank you. I'm not going to eat that . . ."

Marcia listened as her student explained that the salad had been very nice and no, she didn't want the paté, which was meat. Yes, some steamed vegetables for the next course would be very nice. No, she wouldn't eat the fish either.

"How very odd of her," said Gilroy, *sotto voce*.

"Oh I don't think so," said Marcia. "I think it's rather admirable."

Despite everything, she really did. The young had wonderful capacities for moral action. Another silver bell was rung and more waiters appeared. Wine glasses were replaced. Shiraz, rich and red, was poured. Marcia tried not to stare at the bead of wine hanging at the corner of Gilroy's mouth. With a quick flick, he licked it back in.

"Delirious," he said.

"I beg your pardon?"

"Delicious."

*

To her right, Daniel retold stories about his college days and Marcia found she was slightly too full and slightly too tight to disentangle herself from the dreary chatter. She nodded and smiled and nodded some more. Silver sliced through pillowy tissues of flesh.

She saw Grace listening with an expression of mild amusement. Those beautiful brown eyes darted to Marcia. Marcia winked, in spite of that nagging sensation in her chest, that ache, like a bone that wants to be broken. She shouldn't have brought her, she thought. She was too young for the Master's Dinner. But this was something she always thought. She would change her mind in a course or two . . .

*

"Darling."

Hélène, tall, imperious Beautiful Hélène, stood half-stooped beside Grace, hand resting lightly on the girl's shoulder. "Are you enjoying your dinner?"

"Oh very much."

"How *wonderful*. And has Marcia told you about our little tradition?"

Marcia lowered her eyes too slowly and caught a glimpse of the confusion skittering across Grace's face. A concatenation of pulses shook her chest and beneath the table she dug her fingernails into the fabric of her dress and into her skin and deeper.

"Tradition?" asked Grace. "No? What tradition?"

"It's just a little *thing* we do," said Hélène, "A game, really. This year we thought it would be nice to do it with *you*... Don't look so worried, you don't have to do anything! Come with me, I'll explain everything."

Her hand had encircled Grace's wrist. Marcia took another sip of wine and nodded reassuringly as her student was led out of the Library and into the corridor. Around the table, glances were exchanged, wine-stained lips murmured, and Daniel ran his fingertips along the tablecloth in anticipation, *tap tap tap*, matching the dull throbbing of their blood.

*

Gilroy dabbed at the sauce on his trouser-leg. The more he dabbed the more the sauce spread, making the worsted fabric blush. Hélène had returned (alone, of course) and now stood at the other end of the table, clinking her glass with a butter-knife.

"Darlings," she said, "We have eaten. We have been merry. The time is upon us. Pray silence for the Master's Delight."

The latch, that secret latch in Marcia's heart, lifted. In keeping with custom, the waiters had been ushered outside (always silent). The curtains had been drawn and the modern electric lights dimmed. Folding his napkin across his trouser-leg, Gilroy rested his hands in his lap. He looked, thought Marcia, like a schoolboy on Prize Day. He looked like a little dog by the begging bowl.

There was a quiet *click*.

They turned their attention to the small wooden door in the northern apse, which was breathing slowly open. Philip emerged, hair pressed down, silken shawl draped about his shoulders – and in his hands he carried that broad brazen platter. It caught the candlelight and shone, and Marcia wondered whether the charwomen who polished it knew what it was for.

At the head of the table, with a scrape and reconfiguration of ligaments, the Master stood.

The Master spoke.

What the Master said was of less consequence than the crinkle in his eyes, and that beneficent expression, which hung, luminous, lambent, on his face. It was a kindness, thought Marcia, that look. It was a consolation.

Circumnavigating the room, Philip served the contents of the platter with metal prongs. A slice here, a slice there. He worked his way around the table. Gilroy's fingers plucked at his trouser-leg. When the platter reached Marcia, Daniel mouthed the words "sterling work" and a slice was laid in front of her. Then another – a treat. She smiled in gratitude, staring at the thin, veiny tissue.

Please, said the Master and gestured for them to begin.

*

A quiet huffing was coming from her nose. Silver scraped against bone china and the other guests began to eat. She stared at her plate.

The meat was darker than she remembered – a purple-grey material that seemed all too eager to curl around her fork. It was delicately cooked, lightly braised. The sinews and cartilage were still faintly discernible. Blood seeped across the plate. Beside her, Gilroy was crying softly into his handkerchief. Between sobs, Marcia thought she could hear him saying Thank You Thank You.

She shuffled the meat onto the tip of her fork, then raised it to her mouth. The touch of flesh on the flesh of her tongue made her throat constrict – but it was always like this, she reminded herself, the first bite was always the hardest. It took a moment for her to adjust to the flavour. She bit down and felt the grain separate between her incisors.

Daniel and Teddy were retching discreetly into their napkins. Someone had begun to whistle. The cold thread of half-chewed meat slithered between her lips.

She saw the Master raise his glass.

Thank you, he said, and the trembling in her fingers lessened. The next mouthful slid in much more easily. It was still sour, she thought, but there at the edge of her palate lingered that familiar fragrant earthiness, that warm, human comfort. She chewed and let the juices wash around her mouth. The huffing from her nose grew louder.

Someone, possibly Philip, had started to laugh in a high-pitched whinny. She remembered the quirk of Grace's lips and the room began to palpitate with thick, muscular contractions.

*

It wasn't fair, she thought, eyeing her final forkful. She knew this was a churlish thought, and ungenerous, but she couldn't help herself. She glanced towards the Master. He had closed his eyes and was leaning back in his chair. His mouth hung slack like an empty sack, his fingers running absently along the back of Hélène's beautiful arm.

Philip had grown breathless from laughing and was recovering by the fireplace. Gilroy's face was buried in his hands, his fingers pulling at the sides of his face as if it were a jar of pickles. Daniel and the others were simply looking at their plates. Marcia thought of Grace standing in the Ladies Cloakroom, staring at the gold-gilt sinks. "It's *obscene*," she'd said, in wonder. Marcia raised her fork and felt tears bead the corners of her eyes. It wasn't fair, she thought again.

She sucked the meat from the tip of her fork and imagined the gentleness of Hélène's hand. She imagined sitting, as Grace had sat, and finding the Beautiful Hélène at her shoulder, her elegant fingers ruffling the silk of her dress. A blessing. She imagined being guided into the corridor, the short, gentle explanation, the appearance of the

Master, and then – her imagination failed her. All she knew was it would be wonderful. Perfect. To have the Master's attention, wholly and completely, and for every second for the rest of her life. It wasn't fair, she thought, that others received his favour. Closing her eyes, she ate her last mouthful and finally, with a loving look down the table, it was over.

*

Grunting, she tumbled into the back of the taxi and gave the driver her address. She had drunk and eaten far too much, but it was Saturday tomorrow and she would have a lie-in. As the car pulled out, and the lights of the Club dimmed, she retrieved her phone from the bottom of her bag and sent a quick message to her husband.

"leaving now x"

She loosened the sash on her dress and the straps of her shoes, then slumped back and watched the London lights blink by. Her phone buzzed.

"You two have a nice time?"

Marcia thumbed her reply, "just me, no grace. me drunk x"

The response, a second later, was a smiley face and three kisses.

She pressed her forehead to the car window and overhead, the moon shimmered like a polished plate. It was a shame Grace had been unable to make it, she told herself. Such a shame, she would say. The Master would tie up any loose ends, she thought, and even now the memories were fading. By morning they would be picked quite clean. There would be moments when she might remember snippets – but only fleshlessly – and next year it would be the same again and the next and the next.

She leant down and massaged her heels. In future, she told herself, she would wear flats.

Cloakroom, 1984

Horton sat sweating in the cloakroom. They were everywhere, he thought. Everywhere. They were crawling up the walls, prising up the floorboards. They had infiltrated every corner of the institution.

He pulled a handkerchief from his pocket and mopped his brow. It came away damp. Dear God, Dear holy God. Unrelenting. Unremitting. He could hear them, even now, seeping into the cracks and crannies of his building.

He pressed his back into the reassuring mass of coats and tried to slow his breathing. Dear God, his heart. He checked his jacket pocket and felt the reassuring bulge of his pill bottle. He shook one out, swallowed it dryly in the darkness. If only he had thought to bring a drink. To wash it down, he told himself. There had been wine at the reception. He should have had the foresight.

At least he'd found a chair. And the coats did something to muffle the noise. Yes, he had somewhere quiet to sit and collect himself. Breathe, he cautioned himself. Slower. Breathe. Dear God. Their faces. His pulse tapped a swift bolero within his wrists.

How long? How long had it been going on? Days? Weeks? He'd been so wrapped up in his work, he hadn't seen the signs. But the cracks had opened now, hadn't they? By God they'd opened. These beastly people were crawling in. They were everywhere. Snapping and snarling. He should have heeded the warnings.

Malcolm, Horton thought with a start. Poor Malcolm had told him. He hadn't listened. He hadn't wanted to believe things had degenerated so far. He'd offered sympathy, of course, but thought it all exaggeration. Dear holy God. If only.

There was a gentle knocking, growing louder. Louder. Someone, some *thing*, was knocking on the cloakroom door. Instinctively, he braced himself against it, forcing the legs of his chair alongside the wooden frame. Go away, he thought. *Go away*. Please Dear God, why won't you just go away. The knocking continued. He would stay quiet, he told himself, "button up", as his father used to say. "Button up," he murmured to himself. Like these jackets, he thought wildly. Buttons. Jackets. The handle of the door began to turn and flap at his shoulder.

"I'm busy!" he blurted out. Ridiculous – what could he be busy with?

"Professor Horton?" It was a woman's voice, of course. "Is that you? We were wondering where you'd disappeared to . . ."

I bet you were, thought Horton bitterly.

"Leave me alone," he muttered. Then again, but louder, "Leave. Me. Alone."

"Are you alright? We just want to talk . . ."

Talk. Yes, that's what they called it. Talking. Malcolm had been right. They gave every indication of being *reasonable*. They drew you in, invited you to "talk", and then they had you. By God, they had you. He lifted his shaking legs and braced himself against the facing wall. The door was locked, he'd made sure of that. He'd pocketed the key. But these creatures were nothing if not persistent.

How had they grown so numerous? he wondered. Oh, he'd been aware something was going on, he'd seen them popping up here and there – like buboes – but he hadn't thought it had spread so far. He should have heeded the signs. But his work – he'd been so wrapped up in his work. And they'd left him in peace. Or so he'd thought. All the while they had been shoring up their grip.

"Professor, won't you come out?"

"Shan't!" The exclamation of a petulant child. He didn't care. They wouldn't listen anyway. They just talked. They talked and talked, with those horrible half-human voices, until they wore you down to nothing. "Horribly persuasive", Malcolm had called them. "They'll worm inside your head and won't come out. They'll eat your thoughts like a maggot in an apple."

Too right, thought Horton, remembering the look on Bancroft's face.

"Join us, Professor, we won't bite," said the woman. "We've got a rather nice Malbec for the reception. Have a glass with us. Please?"

Horton gritted his teeth. He'd be damned if he would. They could have a bloody Chateau Lafite and it wouldn't make a blind bit of difference. He was staying put. He was a rock. He was a boulder. He was the truth, he was Reason. He was Horton, an unchanging, unimpeachable law of logic, an Archimedean point, the last bastion of common sense in a world overrun. They could talk all they wanted, he wouldn't budge. He'd seen what happened to those who did. Hugo Bancroft. That hollow look. Those empty eyes, as if the man had been scooped out from the middle. These beasts, they looked like normal people until they didn't.

"I shan't talk to you any more," he muttered, "so you may as well just go away."

"You're overreacting", came the reply. He remembered her now. She was one of the new ones, a dusky young thing, charming before you saw the poison in her eyes. Hemlock, he thought grimly, has the prettiest flowers.

". . . We're not *monsters*," she was saying, "I'm sure we can find some common ground. There's enough room for everyone, isn't there?"

It was this proprietary attitude of theirs that appalled him the most. What right did they have to any of this? These buildings had sheltered him for longer than many of them had been alive. These were *his* rooms, he thought, *his* home. He felt a tightness in his chest and felt again for his pills before realising it was anger that made his heart constrict, that tautened the worn elastic of his guts. They were insatiable. Damn their eyes, he hated them. That moment was the closest he came to unlocking the door. Reason, blessed reason held him back. He would not part with any part of his mind. With Malcolm and Hugo gone, he was alone.

The voice whispered through the keyhole. "Come out, Professor. There's nothing to be afraid of–"

"I'm not afraid," he barked, despite himself.

"No, of course not," came the reply. "Still, I'm sure it all feels rather *overwhelming*. This *change*. But if you'll talk to us, you'll see we're not so bad. We just want what's best for everyone . . ."

Beasts, he railed to himself, they were nothing more than *beasts*. He clenched his jaw, his fists, the knuckles of his toes. He wouldn't talk. They couldn't make him. He would wait them out. He was an unshakeable law of logic. An Archimedean point. He was Reason. There was more shuffling on the other side of the door and lowered voices. Then the woman spoke and he heard again, or thought he heard, a giggle.

"Professor, there's someone here to talk to you."

A pause, then a muffled sound against the door.

"Richard? Is that you, old boy?"

Fear, wet, cold fear, shivered through his chest. It was Hugo. Or what was left of him. The man's voice was changed. It was breathless somehow, thinner, as if carried from a distance. Dear holy God, they'd hollowed him out. They'd hollowed him out like a briar pipe and all his words were smoke. "Richard," the thing was saying, "Richard, stop playing silly buggers and open the door. I promise, they're not so bad. They're really rather sensible when you get down to it . . ."

Horton pressed his fingers into his ears. "Leave me alone," he muttered. "Why won't you just bloody leave me alone?" He found himself standing and edging back into the embrace of hanging coats. "*Leave me alone.*" The jackets were piled several layers deep and it took him some time to work his way towards the wall. By the time he felt plaster at his back the voices were almost completely muffled. Thank God. He stood beside what felt like a fur stole and breathed a wheezy sigh of relief. He wasn't safe – not yet – but safer.

The door handle was rattling again. He could hear the dull *thump thump thump*. He heard them call, "Professor! Are you okay?" Fire licked his heart. *You beasts*, he thought. He pressed himself against the wall, pushing past tweed and velvet, velour and plastic.

By his ankles he felt a curl of cool air. Odd, he thought. Unexpected. He extended a trembling hand towards the floor. Yes, there was an unmistakeable draught. Hampered slightly by the press of coats, he worked his way along, following the skirting board. It took forever to reach the facing wall, but once there he felt the draught blow stronger. The thing and the woman were a distant murmur now, but the *thump thump thump* of the handle and his heart persisted.

Breathe, he told himself. A puff of mildewed air blew up his trouser leg. He reached a hand into the darkness and found – *nothing*. Where the cloakroom wall should be, there was a hole. His fingers traced the frame of ancient brickwork. It crumbled at his touch. The darkness within, a darkness richer even than the black of velvet coats, beckoned him. Relief, he felt. This was his place. These were his walls. This building, his home, had offered him its protection

– and into the man-shaped hole, Professor Richard Horton slithered.

*

It was surprising how much food one could find within the walls of 17 Mordell Square – surprising, at least, to newcomers to those hidden spaces. Horton, however, had been living within the walls for some time now. He could not say exactly how long – the hours passed differently when one existed on a two-dimensional plane – but over the last few days, weeks, months, years he had become strong and long in arm. He had grown a fulsome beard. He had never grown a beard before and always imagined it would be a flyaway thing, but the mass of hair that now hung from his chin was thick and vital. Whether this was related to his new diet was unclear.

With regular staccato grunts, he pursued a crab-like passage behind the gentlemen's washroom, ever watchful of the pipework.

There were the rodents, of course, but eating rats and mice was a fussy business and a poor economy. They were hoarders and a cannier move was to find the tangles of lint they called nests and to take a share of whatever it was they foraged: crisps, the corners of sandwiches, even, on a rare occasion, a chocolate bar. Horton was always careful to leave enough for them to continue their work. They nipped at him, occasionally, as tenants do, but were otherwise well-behaved.

And water? Well, that was straightforward. He had long ago learned where the pipes dripped and where the couplings were loose. There had been some difficult days when he had mistaken the inflow and outflow pipes – but he had survived. Since finding the hot water tank sandwiched behind Seminar Room 4 he had even begun to take baths.

Needless to say, it had been hard at first. How could it not have been? The darkness, the constant coughing, the fear of spiders in unwanted places. But after a time his eyes had adjusted. He had learned to breathe shallow, subtle breaths and more recently his beard had begun to filter out the cobwebs and flakes of plaster. The spiders still crawled about his body, but he minded them less now, had even begun to grow fond of them.

He was, in many ways, more comfortable within the walls than he had ever been outside them. He pulled himself up the slats beside the central staircase, and felt nothing but gratitude for the building that housed him and hid him and met his needs so capably. There were even a number of well-placed peepholes – behind ceiling-roses, light-switches and skirting-boards – through which he could monitor the comings and goings of those who now roamed the departmental corridors. It was towards one of these, an aperture in a coat-rack by the secretary's desk, that he was at this moment creeping.

Following his departure, they had proliferated. Teeth gritted, he had watched as new appointments had been made and old appointments severed. They had taken over. He no longer thought of them as beasts but a fungoid presence, blooming its way down the corridors. His veins wriggled at the thought of it. The infestation.

Arriving at the departmental office he pressed a dry eyeball to the hole and saw a female tapping at her computer. He blinked. Did he know this one? It was hard to tell. They all moved with those same odious movements, all spoke with that same breathless piping, like broken reeds catching the wind. And the laughter. By God, how he hated their laughter.

As he watched, another figure entered the room. "Professor Leight," said the female and beneath his beard Horton's jaw twitched. He strained and caught a glimpse of Jeremy Leight placing a folder on the desk. Through the plasterboard he could hear the murmur of mild pleasantries and Jeremy's faint chuckles. But of course it wasn't Jeremy. This was a carbon-copy of the man he'd known. This thing moved *differently*. It spoke *differently*. Those eyes though, Horton could never get used to those empty eyes. It had been the same with Hugo and Malcolm and Henry and Philip. One by one, hollowed out and filled with whatever deadly breath propelled the others.

His hand slipped into his pocket and his fingers fastened around the handle of his scissors. He was growing stronger, he told himself. He would not have to wait much longer. Nicked by the metal, blood beaded at his fingertips.

Worse than these hollow creatures were the survivors. The ones who still remembered. Every so often, Horton would see them scuttling down the corridors or crying in the toilet cubicles. He felt no compassion for these broken men who had lacked the wit or courage to escape. In due course, he would release them from their misery. He dragged a spider from his beard and pressed it between his lips. Popping, it released its fluffy liquids. He was growing stronger. It would not be long before he re-emerged.

Plaster rattled around him as he rolled his shoulders. The female looked over, but saw nothing, nothing but the bare white wall. He was growing stronger. His new home had forced his once hunched body to stand upright, to grow taller. His spine had repositioned itself, his muscles growing sinewy and tight. His fingers were vice-like now and could bend and even crack the rusty pipework that ran through the bricks. He was a rock, an unchanging law of logic. He would be a fatal objection.

The sound of their laughter grew faint as Horton crept down the slats and deeper, deeper, deeper into his building . . .

*

Impossibly, his beard grew longer.

He was lying now beneath the floorboards of the faculty common room, inspecting a gas-tap. Overhead, shoe soles shuffled, sprinkling the back of his head with dust. A pair of moccasins, size 6-and-a-half were tapping an adagio over his shoulders. He hated moccasins (of any colour) and hated (so much more) the creature that wore them. The pipework rang softly beneath his lengthening fingernails. He was experimenting.

There was an odd smell lingering beneath the common room. It was not *his* smell – a briny musk – but rich and strangely sweet. He wondered idly if it had something to do with the markings he had noticed by the boiler-room on the second floor. He had spotted them some time ago. They were too big to have been formed by rats, and peculiarly tidy in their arrangement. Scratched into the brickwork, sometimes, somehow, he thought he understood them.

He gave the gas-tap a speculative twist. There was a grudging *croak* – success – and he relaxed his grip. Overhead, the moccasins shuffled, nervously. "Hello?" the creature murmured overhead. Sliding on his stomach, Horton reached the junction at the foot of the wall and began to climb. He peered at the creature through a crack in the mantel. Its gaze flitted around the room, but he knew it saw nothing. Blank, white-washed office walls that contained: drainage, ventilation, radiator pipes, chimney flues, telephone lines, circuitry – all of which Horton now managed with minute and careful control. Woodlice danced between his toes. His ungainly shoes, Oxfords size 10, had been long ago discarded.

He had discovered subtler ways to exert his influence than scissors.

He breathed and the lights flickered. Eyeball pressed to the mantel, he watched as the creature moved uneasily towards the door. "Who's there?" it asked. It sensed him but could not sense him. He breathed through the brickwork and the creature turned. "Marcia?" it asked. But Marcia was nowhere to be seen. He had told her to *leave*.

The mechanism by which the departmental doors were locked was a remarkably simple one. The keys, the pins, the tumblers, the springs all made a certain intuitive sense to him, and his mastery of them had grown quick and precise. He no longer even needed to be in the same room to trigger them – though at times, like now, he liked to watch. He pressed his feathery lips to the wall and whispered in a voice that once sounded like his own.

"*I just want to talk.*"

He saw the fear in the creature's eyes as it turned and scrabbled at the handle – and he could hear it, almost *feel* it, *thud thud thudding* in its socket and the *thud thud thudding* of its heart. "Who's there," the creature asked again – and Horton replied, louder this time, in that voice, which was brittle and underused, but still clear like cracked glass,

"*I am not a monster.*"

*

He was curled around his boiler, limbs pressed into the soft cladding. He rarely moved these days. He could still feel them scurrying around the building, tripping up and down the stairs, but their movements no longer disturbed him. They were like the spiders that crawled across his pale human skin. It was strange to think he had once been so frightened of them. He flexed and the building flexed with him. He sighed and the chimneys breathed out gouts of soot.

He understood the markings now. Scratched by a familiar hand into the copper pipework, they said, You are the grid in which others live. They said, You are the boundary. You are the point from which perspective flows. He had long ago realised there was no need to leave his home in the walls. He burrowed deeper into the insulation, breathing in the musty fibres. Familiar. He was foundational, he thought, he was the fundament. He was the premise and the conclusion. He was a logical necessity, a truth which could not be denied.

His beard had woven itself through the fibres of the cladding.

He had always, ever since his childhood, loved the nooks and crannies, the corners and nests. As a boy, his favourite games had been hide-and-seek and Sardines, though he hated to be found. The crawl-space was his refuge. It was the centre around the centre. It was the shell. The skin is also an organ. The skin will shed. It will peel off.

It will slough to the wind. I will be reborn. I am the fundament, he thought, I am the argument. I am the conclusion. I will house you.

And thinking these things, long in limb and with a peaceful heart, the creature that was once Professor Richard Horton clung to the cladding of the boiler, closed his eyes and when he slept, he dreamed the most wonderful of dreams.

The Empty Man IV: Abbie (2018)

"...top-deck... yeah top-deck... yeah there's a seat over there–... no no not there– ... yeah this one... it's not that there was anything wrong with it I just– ...I just didn't want to sit next to– ...the guy with the hood I mean who wears a hood on a bus? ...yeah creepy exactly ...pervert... and the front is nice isn't it it's like a rollercoaster and you get a different perspective on– ...on everything *exactly*... god I love London I love it *so much* you're so lucky you can walk to uni I wish *my* parents had a spare flat on the– ...oh I mean... oh sorry... no sorry I *know* they're– I didn't mean to– ...no it was a shitty thing to say I'm sorry I know they're a trigger... yeah... yeah... yeah and that's what this evening's about... you me and some *vino* ...no Beth no Finn haha... no it's not far not far at all it's just on Camden Road but ooh did I tell you we're looking to rent a place in Bloomsbury next year so we'll be *neighbours*...I know right I *know* you have to come round *all the time* I mean *all the time* I'll buy you slippers ha ha you can wear them when you come to visit... yeah it's going to be me and Finn obviously and Sarah and Alex ...exactly once she's recovered from the– ...I know I know *so horrible*... but no not Reyna... no... no I mean I *like* her I like her a lot but I don't think– ...yeah I don't think

I could live with her because– ...don't get me wrong she's fun and everything but– ...yeah well *exactly* you *have to* if you're going to *live* with someone and we're just not you know what's the word we just don't *click* you know how some people just *click*... yeah ... *exactly* that's *exactly* what I was thinking when I met you I was like oh my god I *know* this person and not like *I know your type* or whatever but I *know* you on a deeper level we have kinship we have a *bond*......*Crunchy Nut Cornflakes!* That's exactly what I'm talking about and I love that we both– ...Right? *Right?* We– ... and Reyna wouldn't *get* that she wouldn't *understand* Crunchy Nut Cornflakes it's not her fault it's not anybody's fault she just doesn't have the same touchstones as me and you and Sarah and Alex and Finn and that's just that's just– ...god I'm so glad you think so too... that's what I'm talking about it's rare to find someone who actually *gets* you ...yeah ...yeah... no I value you *so much* you're an amazing person you're– ...no *you're* a queen and by the way if Beth can't see that– ...well exactly she can go fuck herself there are plenty of other fish in the lesbian sea can I say that? Ha ha yeah exactly some of my best friends are– ...no no– ...that's what I mean Reyna wouldn't get that joke she'd think I was being homophobic and you know I'm not being homophobic and you're actually gay and you're laughing because you understand the context and context is so important and obviously it's not her fault but she just doesn't get *context* she takes everything so literally so when she hears something that could be *construed* as problematic it's just problematic to her and she goes off on one of her– ...tirades isn't the right word but you know what I mean and I'm not saying you shouldn't be angry about– ...yeah *obviously* you should be angry about systemic racism and oh my god *all* systems of oppression I organised a fucking conference on it but you have to be able to pick out what's *actually* racist and what just *sounds* racist it's an important distinction otherwise you end up– ...exactly and that's another thing– ...that's another reason why I can't live with her because you have to explain *all the jokes* and I mean *all the time* and it's not natural no natural isn't the right world– ...*naturalistic fallacies* ha ha exactly... what I mean is it's not *organic* you have to stop and talk her through it and nothing kills a joke like an explanation... no ha ha no I haven't told her about the flat yet... how come? ... did she say something to you? well to be honest it's a little arrogant if she's just *assuming* she's going to live with us I mean I don't know her *that* well... she's a friend but she's not like a *good* friend not like you or Sarah or Alex or Finn obviously she's a friend... well yeah and I don't mean to sound– ...but I think she thinks we're *better* friends than we actually are I mean I only ever really see her in lectures and seminars and afterwards in the pub and I've met up with her a few times but always with other people it's not like we're you know *bosom buddies* ha ha yeah not *best*-friends and I know she's been having a hard time recently but haven't we all? And it's not like it's *my* responsibility to take care of her I don't have to be friends with everyone it's not my job to take *everyone* under my wing there's only so much of me to give and anyway it would be what's the word what's the word I'm looking for... *inauthentic*... yeah de Beauvoir... exactly I can't fabricate a bond out of nothing there has to be some *shared understanding* or *reciprocity* or whatever– ... yeah I knew you'd get it I knew you would– ...I said the same thing to Morgan and she said I was being *exclusionary* no she didn't say it explicitly she *implied* it but I'm not excluding anyone I invited her to my party didn't I? I just don't want to *live* with her and there are plenty of other people she can live with it doesn't have to be me... yeah... yeah... and that's *exactly* what I'm talking about... yeah *thank you* for understanding I love that I can talk to you about this stuff and there's no judgement it's a safe space... no *you're* my safe space ha ha... *right?* Because it's not about race *obviously* it's not about race but if you take what I'm saying *literally* then it might *seem* like it's about race or ethnicity but it's just about shared culture or whatever... it's like when I meet someone jewish we have the same points of reference the same–...yeah yeah... and there's just less *overlap* with her and that's fine isn't it it's just fine it's all about *context*–...huh? ...what no we don't need to get off no not yet... no no I think it's on diversion we're just going round the houses yeah *literally* round the houses haha... yeah right– ... and Reyna's so *earnest* about it about learning all the *idioms* and I don't want to go on about it but– ... her little book is cute and everything but it's kind of exhausting too you know? Every time I hang out with her it's like I have to do a director's commentary and I can't *live* like that I need a space where I can relax where I can say stuff without worrying that what I'm saying will be– ...exactly or *misinterpreted* that's it she's always listening she's always asking questions like the other day we were sitting in the common room and–...god ha ha I'm repeating myself I forgot I told you about that but you know what I mean? She just sits there and talks about what people are saying and whether or not it's– ... yeah if I hear the word *problematic* one more time I'm going to–...and look I get it I understand that we have to be careful with language fuck I know we have to be careful I've read Irigaray and–...exactly I *know* but we can't just start from scratch we need to be able to *communicate* and if you focus on the little things too much you end up actually creating obstacles to *meaningful dialogue* and I'm not being mean but Reyna can come across as a little ...ha ha paranoid *yeah* I'm glad you said it it's the right word she's always listening for *connotations* and that's important *obviously* but I can't *live* like that I need *down time* too I need to switch off it's a question of *self-care*... like that complaint did you hear about her complaint? ...oh maybe it's confidential ha ha... top secret... but I'm sure it's fine if I– ... yeah and you're *trustworthy* everyone knows you're trustworthy... and I'm sure Marcia was going to mention it to you anyway–...well *apparently* Reyna raised a complaint about–...

no... no no not about anyone in particular– ... no not *him* though that would make sense he's such a pervert but it wasn't him it was about the *department as a whole*... can you imagine the entire *department*? She said it was *hostile* no that wasn't the word she used but it was something like that... and I get that there are some *unpalatable elements* mentioning no names cough cough *Grover* but come on the *whole department* I mean apart from anything else it doesn't make *metaphysical* sense ha ha– ... Anyway Marcia was doing an *informal* assessment and you know that we're close– ... yeah Marcia's fun she's super fun– ... and she asked me if I thought the department was *hostile* or whatever the word was– ... I think she asked me specifically because she knows I've got an interest in– ...exactly... and I don't mean to sound arrogant but I am actually quite important in the social life of the department– ... anyway she asked me *off the record* and I was like yeah obviously some of the men in the faculty are creeps but it's also one of the most progressive departments in the–...exactly if not the *world* ...and I've certainly never found it *hostile* and definitely not in the way Reyna means... and it doesn't help– ...what's that? No no don't worry it's still on diversion we'll get there eventually the driver would make an announcement if there was a change to the route... ha ha yeah well that's what happens if you take taxis everywhere ha ha... anyway where was I? I just think Reyna was overreacting and it's pointless trying to raise a complaint against the *entire* department plus it's a waste of energy and potentially destructive because these aren't the people we need to be fighting these aren't the people– ... right? Using words like *hostile* or *dangerous* just makes her sound– ...yeah and *over-sensitive* and that doesn't help when– ... exactly and I'm sorry but I *do* think she's overreacting I do yeah I do because obviously *all* institutions have their issues sure I agree but we're definitely better than most and– ... well yeah... yeah... *yeah*... Anyway can you *imagine* what it would be like if you had to listen to her going on about that twenty-four-seven if you had to live with that non-stop morning till night there'd be no break... I can't I couldn't- ...no no thank *god*... no I haven't seen her in a while not since last week actually so the topic hasn't come up and ha ha yeah I'm not going to raise it am I? I mean maybe if she- ... but probably not... if I'm lucky she's just- ...ha ha you're so *dark* I love it... I love it... only you could make a joke like that- ...hang on- ... I'm just- ...hey you know what... I think we *might* have taken the wrong bus because I don't recognise any of this but maybe we should get off at the next stop because that guy is still staring at us yeah the guy with the hood ..."

Mycorrhizae

For the life of her, Margaret Munroe could not remember who had brought her the plant. There was not much she *could* remember these days, she thought wearily as she dusted its stubby little leaves. People were always saying how *lucid* she was but she knew, even if they didn't, how much she had forgotten and was in the process of forgetting. Words mainly. Words. The other day she had been talking to that girl Samantha and had completely forgotten the word for – well, for whatever it had been. She had been able to remember *nominal dysphasia* but had lost any trace of the ordinary word for whatever the thing had been. "Lucid my ass" as the Americans would say. She dipped the strip of Kleenex in her glass and wiped the stem of the plant. She had better hearing than her visitors realised. She would listen to them as they talked in overly earnest whispers outside her door. They were always saying how impressive it was that yadayadayada and every so often they would allude to the smell. She gave the plant a sip of water and held it up to the light. Wherever it had come from she had grown fond of it, this little green friend of hers. She didn't like to have favourites, as her children could attest, but of all the plants standing along her cracked, sun-bleached windowsill, she had a particular affection for this ugly little thing in its cheap plastic pot. There was something curiously defiant about it. It wasn't showy, not like the orchids, nor needy like the umbrella, nor so defensive as the trio of purple blossoming cacti. It had no flowers, no discernible odour, never seemed much to grow, drank little and yet it persisted. She placed it back on the windowsill beside the others, then hauled herself to her armchair. Samantha was arriving in an hour and she wanted to have a nap so she would be "lucid" when the girl arrived.

Girl was wrong, Margaret told herself when she woke. Samantha was a woman in her late thirties or early forties. Still, one could be an *old girl*, couldn't one? Paul was often calling her *old girl. Old girl* this, *old girl* that. There was something charming about it, she thought, not that she would say so to Samantha who like most of the young people these days was very concerned with what they called "the politics of everyday language". Not that Samantha was really a young person. A young person comparatively speaking, she thought. She wiped the gunky residue from the corners of her mouth and arranged herself in her armchair, flattening down her skirt. When had she last urinated? She had better relieve herself before Samantha arrived – it took such a damnably long time and she didn't want to interrupt the session. She pulled herself out of her chair and began the arduous affair of what her father in his lighter moods would call *going widdle.* I go widdle, you go widdle, it goes widdle, he would say. We go widdle, you plural go widdle, they all goeth widdle. By the time Margaret had finished widdling, Samantha had let herself in and was on hand to help her back to her armchair. Margaret patted the girl on the hand, *thank you my dear,* which was the most she could manage by way of physical affection these days. Samantha boiled the kettle and produced a cup of very weak tea for Margaret and a cup of very strong coffee for herself. Then the session began. Margaret enjoyed the session, as she always did. Of course, there was something slightly morbid about it, as with any attempt to document a life and a life's work before it had quite ended, but it was enlivening too. These were memories to which Margaret had easy access and even when she didn't she was able to make things up and not be questioned. And yes, it was true, there was something gratifying about being the centre of a research project albeit a small and poorly funded one.

*

There had been something Samantha had said during the session that had irritated Margaret. But what? She watched the girl pack up her rucksack and rinse her empty coffee cup. Margaret's own milky tea sat half-finished on the coffee table. What had she said? It didn't matter, she thought as she waved Samantha goodbye, watched the door open and close and heard the latch click shut. It didn't matter what she'd said. It didn't matter – and yet the knot of irritation remained there in her chest, a tangle, a tightness. Was it irritation or heartburn, she wondered. Was she dying? Yes. But slowly. Sometimes these days she could go for almost a minute without breathing. She could sit in her armchair, not moving, not holding her breath exactly, just *still*. This, she imagined as she took a shallow breath and then, eventually, another, was how it would feel. All of her bones, all of her organs, everything seemed to rattle slightly. Her hips had stopped aching, but she knew that when she stood, they would start again. But what was it that Samantha had said? Whatever it was it had gotten under her skin. Gotten. Got. It had got under her skin. No, it had *gotten* under her skin, which was easy enough these days, she thought, as she looked at the backs of her wrinkled hands. How had she grown so old? She clenched the arms of her armchair and pulled herself upwards and for a second stood, pendulously, hunched, knees bent, vibrating slightly. She felt lightheaded and lowered herself back onto the seat, which welcomed her with its overly familiar embrace. It was often like this after Samantha's visits. She was drained, as if the girl had taken something by force, though of course she hadn't. Margaret sipped at her tea, took another, deeper breath, and thus fortified pushed herself out of her chair and went to the bathroom to go widdle.

If anything the knot in her chest was growing tighter. Still vibrating, she made her way back to the windowsill and slowly lowered herself onto the seat of her walker. It didn't matter what Samantha had said, she told herself, and picking up the spray released a thin, luminous mist over the plants. Water droplets beaded the pane behind them, forming rivulets that ran into the chips in the paint and grooves of the frame. She needed to relax, she told herself, she needed to breathe. The knot in her chest turned. Unravelling? Maybe. She picked up the stubby plant in its cracked plastic pot and cradled it in her lap, spilling a small but inconsequential amount of soil on her– on her– on her– *nightie*. Her *nightie*. Had she been wearing her nightie the whole time? It didn't much matter, it was unlikely Samantha would have noticed and even less likely she would have cared. One of the benefits of old age is that others hold you to much lower standards. Much. Far. Much. She stroked the fleshy leaves of the plant feeling or perhaps imagining the softness of their silvery hairs, spines which served as a disincentive to smaller, hungrier, more sensitive creatures. She squinted. She knew there were even smaller beings, against whom the hairs offered no protection, beings that were even now migrating from her own semi-translucent skin onto the plant's epidermal layer, passing others travelling in the opposite direction, from plant to Margaret, to take up residence along with thousands more in the folds and the creases of her finger-webs. *Staphylococcus*. Why were these words so much easier to remember than others? The knot was growing hotter in her chest. Not painfully, she thought, quite the opposite in fact though this in itself was unnerving. She blinked. Refocused. Heat. A pleasant sort of heat. Dizziness. She felt the loving, microbial exchange blossom beneath her fingertips, and the interface between organisms dissolve as minuscule flora and fauna intermingled, making fun of organismic boundaries which were, as Margaret had always believed, vague enough to be meaningless. Whatever Samantha had said it did not, could not, controvert the thought that the concept of an organism like the concept of a species was a construct, a heuristic, a useful heuristic certainly, but a heuristic nonetheless, that did little to capture the interconnections between this living thing and that living thing and those living things over there. She felt the heat burn down her left flank and along her leg but continued to stroke the plant and felt, strangely, as though she was herself being stroked. How very odd. It was not unpleasant, neither for her nor for the plant. Was there anything to tell between the two? It was not unpleasant to feel the sunlight through the windowpane, to feel the coolness of the soil, the prickle of the air, to feel those magical, pulsing, ancient photons splashing into her like silver rain, piercing the chlorophyll sacs that sat stacked in the thylokoids, in the grana, in those most precious of plastids the chloroplasts, splitting water molecules, sending hydrogen ions flying, oxygen bubbling, photoexcitation causing beautiful, kaleidoscopic eruptions of energy, which shivered in her leaves, while down below, down below, her roots wriggled in the pleasure and the silence of the soil ...

*

"Hello old girl," a familiar face smiled at her from her bedside. "You've had quite a turn, haven't you?"

Where was she? The man was at her bedside so she must be in her bed. She tried to turn but found her head strapped in place. No, not strapped, she thought, but rooted. She was lying on her right-hand side with a view of this familiar man, unable to turn or twist herself or wipe the gunk from her lips or stretch the ache out of her shoulders. At another time this might have worried her. The familiar man was talking to her in his familiar way – *old girl* this, *old girl* that – and she remembered without necessarily wanting to remember that she had slept with him, a long time ago. It had been an awkward encounter. They'd been greener limbed but the vascular processes by which they'd exchanged fluids had been stuttered and inefficient, and neither of them had spoken of it since, at least not while sober. She blinked the memory away. She could still blink, she noticed, though her eyelids were sticky and her lashes clumped. The familiar man was trying to explain what had happened, how she'd fallen, but there was something dysfunctional occurring in the osmotic process by which understanding passes from one being to another. She was saturated. *Margaret* he kept saying, *Margaret*. And she remembered that this Margaret was *her*. Professor Margaret Munroe – this was her. Except it wasn't, not quite. Electrons shivered within her, mitochondria pulsed and swirled. Mitchondrial DNA is matrilineal. Where was she? In her bed. But also watching her bed from the windowsill. She was *spatially extended*. She was *discontinuous*. She was surprisingly untroubled by this, though she realised as well that she was decaying. Those tiny pneumatic systems, those living pumps that strained inside her, were slowing down. The once-plump capillaries were struggling and failing. Soon, she thought, the rot would set in and her extremities would start to shrivel and fall off. The same realisation appeared to have dawned on the familiar man, who was licking his lips in a way that was less than erotic. She could not understand why he was so worried when she herself was not in the least bit afraid. She knew how it worked; the leaching, the break-up and fragmentation, the microbial bloom. There was nothing there to fear; the line between the living and the dead was as blurred as the line between this thing and that thing and all the rest. Outside the sky shone a cheerful blue, and whether it was through intent or heliotropic instinct her palm opened slightly to catch a thread of sunlight. She was not afraid. It was a nice surprise, here at the end, to realise that she believed everything she had ever written.

*

The familiar man was still there when she woke, smiling at her. "...Do you remember when–" And in fact, in this instance, she *did* remember when. She remembered standing at that podium, just as he described it, talking in the way she once did, which is to say– which is to say– which is to say– *effortlessly*. Yes, that was the word. *Effortlessly*. She remembered the audience, she remembered the subject. She remembered how in her parting notes she had introduced what she had sententiously called a *new modelling method for capturing biological data*... She remembered, with a fibrillation of pleasure that travelled down to her roots, the expectant expressions on the faces of the assembled researchers, those people who had admired her once – if that was the word, *admired* – as she'd leant down behind the podium to retrieve this clever model of hers, elegantly simple in design, and eminently portable. She'd placed it on the mantel of the podium. It had been a joke, of course, a wry nod to the impossibility of doing what it was that she did and the audience had laughed appreciatively. It was a pot-plant, a hyacinth bought from the local supermarket. *The perfect representation of biological data*. The familiar man chuckled at the memory of the phrase and patted her hand – and Margaret might have died, if that was the word, quite happily had not the handle of the door turned and a girl – no, a woman – stepped in.

The woman slipped her rucksack from her shoulders and stepped forwards to lean over and graft a kiss onto Margaret's palsied cheek. She squeezed Margaret's arm and Margaret experienced   what did one call it? A difficult feeling, an acrid feeling, a feeling like the sting of tiny mandibles dissolving plant flesh. A moment earlier she had been ready to submit herself, her lignin, her cellulose, her hemicellulose, to the beautiful and baroque processes of decomposition. Now, however, she felt– she felt– well whatever that feeling was, that elusive feeling which ached like salt in the soil. The girl was smiling, cheeks flushed and buoyant with the water of youth. She liked coffee, Margaret remembered. A cup of strong black coffee, a diuretic which would suck the water from her very veins. *Lucid my ass*. What was that feeling? It lingered. It burrowed. Her other parts, which were arranged neatly along the windowsill, withered slightly. She realised that she did not want to be preserved. No, she wanted the detritivores to settle on her, to render dust unto dust so that she might contribute in her small but tangible way to the nutritive cycle. She did not want to be preserved, yet this is what the woman, the girl, the young person had promised and Margaret knew too well how it worked. She knew the milky process by which her weak, fibrous body would be ground down, and pumped and pulped and spread into infinitesimally thin sheets to dry. She did not want this. She did not want to be reduced to a slim sheaf of dead-matter, saturated in toxins, preserved in plastics, peppered with burnt black ink, and bound in burning unguent. She did not want this. Straining, she turned her human head and tried to form a string of human words but succeeded only in stretching the thin, febrile skin across her lips into the simulation of a– of a– of a smile. The woman, the girl, smiled back and, squeezing her unresisting hand, assured Margaret that there was nothing she could do to stop them, the girl, the familiar man, from performing that ancient and terrible procedure by which a living being, with living thoughts, is transformed into a book, a book very much like the one you may well be holding right now in your warm and fleshy hands.

A Manifesto for Horror As Critique of Analytic Philosophy

Horror is the perfect foil for analytic philosophy. Where the latter revels in scientistic precision and the "rigours of logic", the former – especially in its weirder manifestations – delights in the supernatural. It corrodes the expectations of logic. Indeed, it is this delight in the illogical that partly constitutes horrific writing. Horror emerges when an audience is deprived of a sensible point of purchase on a narrative (real or imagined). Where analytic philosophy aspires to a close and careful analysis of phenomena, horror pointedly resists it. In this, the genre dreams many of the same unsettling dreams as the deconstructionists – and it is for this reason, perhaps, that the analytic philosophers of the early 90s were so unnerved at the prospect of J.D.'s honorary doctorate at Cambridge. To the awarding body, they wrote the following lines:

> "In the eyes of philosophers, and certainly among those working in leading departments of philosophy, the bastard's work does not meet accepted standards of clarity and rigour."

This is the only printable passage from the letter submitted to the Board, which otherwise consists of a series of expletives about J.D.'s parentage.

The Horrific Philosopher attempts to examine the rhetorical, methodological and critical potential of horror in relation to analytic philosophy and its associate schools of thought. The Horrific Philosopher offers an alternative canon of Torture Experiments (more commonly, "Thought Experiments") to run alongside the Analytic Imaginary critiqued by M.l.D and M.l.C.. These are stories in which analytic philosophers (including Horrific Philosophers) are themselves implicated. Analytic readers will (I hope) be duly horrified by the canker that sits at the heart of their discipline.

By "analytic philosophy", I am talking about a particular brand of anglophone thought that emerged out of a culture dominated primarily by white, male British academics working at the start of the twentieth century. B.A.W.R, G.E.M and then subsequently, P.F.S., A.J.A. and their cadre at Oxford and Cambridge. Great fleas have lesser fleas upon their backs. Much ink has been spilled (by analytic philosophers) trying to define the x, where x is analytic philosophy. I am not myself especially concerned about the necessary and sufficient conditions for what makes the mysterious x an analytic philosopher – nor, I think, should you be, unless it is to prevent yourself becoming x. Anyone who is embedded deeply enough within the discipline to worry about it has, I think, a general understanding of who the perpetrators are. Anyone who is outside the discipline is probably better off not knowing.

Having said this, there are certain features of analytic philosophy that are worth mentioning in a Manifesto that aims to unsettle it. Having trained in the discipline at undergraduate, doctoral and postdoctoral levels, and having dreamed about it for much longer, I am almost painfully well-placed to offer some insight into its society and habits – and the forms of discursive and physical violence it perpetuates.

Analytic philosophy is a rot in the brain. It is a condition not dissimilar to *witzelsucht*, the curious pathology characterised by a tendency to make puns or to tell long and boring stories. Related to these peculiar semantic symptoms is the analyst's fetish for logical notation. Consider the following quotation offered to us by D.F. in his commentary on *Mind and Power*:

> "... Never has there been a sterner reproach to the age-old adage, $(a =_f b)$ & *not* $(a =_g b)$ & $(g(a) \vee g(b))$ & $(g(a)$ & not $g(b)) \ldots$"

One recoils from this reduction of a living language to a series of bracketed beans; it is an attitude all the more shocking given the beautiful if Piranesian phrasing found in *Mind and Power* itself. Even the lighter, more accessible contributions to the tradition exhibit these analy*tics*, these uncontrollable convulsions of brains calmly bludgeoned by set-squares. Analytic philosophy is famously intolerant of ambiguity and metaphor; it revels in literalism.

Analytic philosophers follow B.A.W.R. in what he called the "divide and conquer" method of conceptual analysis. Phenomena and problems should be broken down into their constituent parts, he writes, so that they may be conquered and subjugated. The analytic philosophers have a fondness for scalpels. Razors. Carving knives. Relatedly, they aspire for "clarity" and "distinctness". They often talk of ideas *percolating*, as though subject to a delicate form of mental distillation. Clarity. Clearness. Transparency. Lucidity. Here again, we see the utility of horrific writing, which neither simplifies nor clarifies. Horror – weird horror in particular – is a frothing excess, a miasma that, unlike B.A.W.R.'s piecemeal analysis can encompass and infest even the most unwieldy of conceptual schemas. When we think of horror, we think less of percolation, than of fermentation. Thoughts are not *clarified*, but rather promulgated. They do not reduce but rather spread. They throb. They bleed and infect. A horror book is a nesting ground for disease. A horror book is a spongiform mass, a fibrous solid, a mucous membrane that wriggles with maggots and worms. Horrific writing is alive with fleas.

Aristotle believed that in the right conditions fleas could spontaneously generate in dust and putrid matter. This is one of the few points of agreement between horrific writers and the old slave master.

What else? The aggressiveness and machismo of the discipline has been well-documented by H.B. and J.S.. The whiteness of the discipline has been examined by K.D. and S.A.. There are some, like S.H., who think these features are to a certain degree accidental; as a way of thinking, analytic reasoning is neither irredeemably White nor Male – and through careful consideration, the thought goes, it may be rehabilitated. In some moods, I agree with her. These words, however, were not written in such a mood. Whether the protagonists of horrific stories know it or not, there is no hope in horror. The stories contained herein align, instead, with K.A.'s incendiary advice: to raze the institution to the ground.

A word or two now about the Horrific Method. Writing can be a long and laborious process. We all have tricks and techniques for making it easier; coffee, for instance, or candles, or cutting the tips of our fingers and intoning the names of philosophical forebears. Fleas sometimes help. These stories have been difficult to write for all sorts of reasons – and I have found it hard to know how to nurture these thoughts and decompose the dead matter.

I, or rather *we*, have re-developed a very old research methodology eminently suitable to horror writing. It is one that would appal analytic philosophers, save perhaps one – C.D.B. – whose essay "The Relevance of Psychical Research to Philosophy" is a rare example of an analytic philosopher attempting to transcribe his nightmares. On reading C.D.B.'s essay, it is hard not to be struck by the critical potential of spirit-gathering within the sphere of academic philosophy. It is through such methods that I contacted my co-authors, whose ideas populate these pages alongside my own. Swarming, blood-sucking multitudinous fleas.

If you are beginning to feel that these words and their author are becoming untethered, we are glad of it. The aspiration of horrific philosophy is to write, like F.W.N., such that no clear line can be drawn between the product of a cogent and a syphilitic mind.

The method that informs the Horrific Philosopher's stories is supra-rational. As C.D.B. discovered, psychical research is innately unrigorous. Both analytic and non-analytic readers may level charges of plagiarism against this Manifesto. They might be right to do so – but the responsibility for this lies at the intangible feet of my co-authors. The process by which I have communed with my collaborators has not been conducive to good citation practices. If those I spoke to have a care for careful referencing, it is not one they shared with me – and while the technologies of channelling have certainly progressed in recent years, they are not yet so advanced as to pass peer-review.

Mediumship as a method creates another worry, which while less effable is more expansive. In speaking to those beyond the veil, and transcribing their thoughts, all conceptual way-markers have been removed. Epistemically speaking, I am corrupted. It is unclear to me whose thoughts have found their way onto this page, and which powers move, and continue to move, through me. A certainty in oneself and one's authenticity: this is an appeal of the analytic method for which I have yearned most earnestly. As a research practice, spirit channelling creates the possibility that one may become dispossessed of oneself. More damaging than this, the very prospect of entertaining another's ideas has a corrosive effect. Whence do these words come? Who possesses them, and whom do they possess?

This complaint manifests differently in different minds. These days it appears to me as an unending buzzing in the hollow of my skull that picks and nips and sucks at the hidden vesicles. Be warned, for whatever else horror writing is, it is certainly not safe for the writers, or readers. In the right conditions even the most dusty words can bring forth life, spontaneous, buzzing, frothing and infinite in a form the human mind cannot compass ...

Appendix I: Recurring Characters

While the author's pencil drawings of his characters are too grotesque to be reproduced here, the editorial team has decided to include a selection of his character notes, which give an insight into the breadth of this fictional world and the relationships he conceived between these recurring figures. – S.K.L.

Daniel Figgis: "(1783–1856, 1888–1931, 1941–) Breathless, grey. Author of *Individuating Items*. Long-time confidante of Almond Gilroy. Student of Paul Wimsey. Fellow of St Bartolph's College, Professor Emeritus B.C., London."

Theodore Barnhoffer: "(1792–1861, 1867–1920, 1949–) Credibly tall. Author of *A Philosopher's Life*, editor of *A Guide to Philosophical Personages*. Self-styled provocateur. Married to Marcia Houghton (1857–1861, 1994–1995). Fellow of St Mervyn's College, Professor Excelsius B.C., London."

Andrew Marvell O'Connor: "(1632–1692, 1758–1801, 1892–1912, 1931–2015) Deceptively interesting. Author of *Mind and Power*. Affianced to Yuko Saito (deceased). Plagiarist. Corduroy-wearer. Contemporary of Theodore Barnhoffer and Paul Wimsey. Associate of Benjamin Sallow. Posthumous Fellow of Bartolph's College."

Paul Wimsey K.B.E.: "(1743–1778, 1821–1886, 1890–1923, 1939–) Pale, rigid, lumpen. Originator of "subjective-objectivism". Knighted for "Services to Metaphysics". Blood-relative to Marcia Houghton, contemporary and friend of Andrew O'Connor. Long fingernails. Professor of Logic at Jerome's College."

Paul Grover: "Cherubic. Department Head at B.C., London. Fond of rings. Member of the Remus Club. Married to Marcia Houghton (1919–1921, 1996–1997), esteemed by Theodore Barnhoffer. Author of *Tractatus Sub-Ethica*."

Benedict Bertrand Bertrand March: "(1634–1681, 1702–1764, 1798–1856, 1899–1938, 1953–) Author of "Campus Rumpus" series (*Socratic Quarterly*) and the academic monograph *Persons and People*. Confidante of Almond Gilroy. Provost of St Mervyn's College. Piccolo player."

Professor Almond Gilroy O.B.E.: "(1740–1770, 1802–1853, 1920–) Stick-like, ashen. Flat-cap in wet weather, cricket hat in warm weather. Editor of *Socratic Quarterly* (1921–2002). Married to Marcia Houghton (1763–1770, 1987–1992) and Alexandria Gordon (1992–1993). Honorary Fellow of St Mervyn's. Member of the Remus Club."

Marcia Houghton: "(1750–1782, 1801–1870, 1890–1913, 1914–1944, 1958–) Overtly generous. Self-styled "progressive". Member of the Remus Club. Department Head at B.C., London. Supervisor to Grace C. (before her disappearance) and Abbie S. (before her disappearance). Volubly reluctant meat-eater."

The Empty Man: "(???) Hollow? Hooded? Veiled? Forgettable? Homophage? Cruel? A question??? Transcendent? Immanent? Inescapable? A function of the bounds of rationality???"

Appendix II: Quotations

The stories compiled in this collection were found in bundles that also included pages of extensive quotations from many of the foundational texts of analytic philosophy (as well as certain "lesser works"). Indeed, much of the author's work was scribbled in the margins or between the lines of these passages and it has taken considerable effort and editorial skill to disentangle his writing from the writings he wrote upon. In a bid to render the stories more readable, the editorial team has separated the two and positioned the less easily digestible, and at times more disturbing material in this appendix. – S.L.K.

Introductory Essay: Uroborotic Horror

"One shade of colour cannot simultaneously have two different degrees of brightness or redness, a tone not two different strengths, etc. And the important point here is that these remarks do not express an experience but are in some sense tautologies. Every one of us knows that in ordinary life. If someone asks us 'What is the temperature outside?' and we said 'Eighty degrees', and now he were to ask us again 'And is it ninety degrees?' we should answer, 'I told you it was eighty.' We take the statement of a degree (of temperature, for instance) to be a *complete* description which needs no supplementation. Thus, when asked, we say what the time is, and not also what it isn't."

–Ludwig Wittgenstein, "Some Remarks on Logical Form"

The Ring of Gyges

"... He was a shepherd in the service of the then king of Lydia, and one day there was a great storm and an earthquake in the district where he was pasturing his flock and a chasm opened in the earth. He was amazed at the sight, and descended into the chasm and saw many astonishing things there, among them, so the story goes, a bronze horse, which was hollow and fitted with doors, through which he peeped and saw a corpse which seemed to be of more than human size. He took nothing from it save a gold ring it had on its finger, and then made his way out. He was wearing this ring when he attended the usual meeting of shepherds which reported monthly to the king on the state of his flocks; and as he was sitting there with the others he happened to twist the bezel of the ring towards the inside of his hand. Thereupon he became invisible to his companions, and they began to refer to him as if he had left them. He was astonished, and began fingering the ring again, and turned the bezel outwards; whereupon he became visible again. When he saw this he started experimenting with the ring to see if it really had this power, and found that every time he turned the bezel inwards he became invisible, and when he turned it outwards he became visible. Having made his discovery he managed to get himself included in the party that was to report to the king, and when he arrived seduced the queen, and with her help attacked and murdered the king and seized the throne ..."

–Plato's *Republic*, Book II (trans. Desmond Lee)

Cousin Vincent

"... every one finds that, whilst comprehended under that consciousness, the little finger is as much a part of himself as what is most so. Upon separation of this little finger, should this consciousness go along with the little finger, and leave the rest of the body, it is evident the little finger would be the person, the same person; and self then would have nothing to do with the rest of the body"

–John Locke, *Essay Concerning Human Understanding*, II.xxvii.19

By which we learn that "Snow is White"

"... the sentence constituted by three words, the first of which consists of the 19th, 14th, 15th, and 23rd letters, the second of the 9th and 19th letters, and the third of the 23rd, 8th, 9th, 20th, and 5th letters of the English alphabet ..."

–Alfred Tarski, "The Semantic Conception of Truth and the Foundations of Semantics"

Empty Man I: The German Logician (1902)

"I have only in the last years really learned to comprehend antisemitism. If one wants to make laws against the Jews, one must be able to specify a distinguishing mark [Kennzeichen] by which one can recognise a Jew for certain. I have always seen this as a problem ..."

–Gottlob Frege, *Diary entry 22nd April 1924*

The Gravesend Institute

"... we have seen what monstrous philosophical edifices have been created by slipping surreptitiously, from the ordinary uses of words to extraordinary uses which are never explained ..."

–C.E.M. Joad, *Essays in Common Sense Philosophy*

A Response to C.D. Baird's Reading of the Pitwell Phenomenon

"If paranormal cognition and paranormal causation are facts, then it is quite likely that they are not confined to those very rare occasions on which they either manifest themselves sporadically in a spectacular way or to those very special conditions in which their presence can be experimentally established. They may well be continually operating in the background of our normal lives. Our understanding of, and our misunderstandings with, our fellow-men; our general emotional mood on certain occasions; the ideas which suddenly arise in our minds without any obvious introspectable cause; our unaccountable immediate emotional reactions towards certain persons; our sudden decisions where the introspectable motives seem equally balanced; and so on; all these may be in part determined by paranormal cognition and paranormal causal influences . . ."

–C.D. Broad, *Religion, Philosophy and*
Psychical Research: Selected Essays

Empty Man II: Theodore (1999)

"[the tradition of British empiricism] is a commonsensical tradition. . . Sticking close to the facts, and close to observation, and not being carried away by German Romanticism, high falutin' talk, obscurity, metaphysics. It's a tradition, on the whole, of good prose. That is very important. If you write good prose, you can't succumb to the sort of nonsense we get from Germany and now also from France."

–A.J. Ayer, "An Interview with A.J. Ayer"

Bare Substrata

"[E]ven though horses, leaves, sun and stars are not inventions or artefacts, still, if such things as horses, leaves, sun and stars were to be singled out in experience at all so as to become the objects of thought, then some scheme had to be fashioned or formed, in the back and forth process between recurrent traits in nature and would-be cognitive conceptions of these traits, that made it possible for them to be picked out."

–David Wiggins, *Sameness and Substance Renewed*

such brittle bodies

"I am apt to suspect negroes and in general all other species of men (for there are four or five different kinds) to be naturally inferior to whites. There never was a civilized nation of any other complexion than white, nor even any individual eminent either in action or speculation. No ingenious manufactures amongst them, no arts, no sciences . . ."

–David Hume, "Of National Characters"

Empty Man III: Marcia (2010)

". . . a performative utterance will, for example, be *in a peculiar way* hollow or void if said by an actor on the stage, or if introduced in a poem, or spoken in soliloquy. This applies in a similar manner to any and every utterance – a sea-change in special circumstances. Language in such circumstances is in special ways – intelligibly – used not seriously, but in ways *parasitic* upon its normal use – ways which fall under the doctrine of the etiolations of language."

–J.L. Austin, How to Do Things with Words

The Locked Room

"... suppose a man be carried, whilst fast asleep, into a room where is a person he longs to see and speak with; and be there locked fast in, beyond his power to get out: he awakes, and is glad to find himself in so desirable company, which he stays willingly in, i.e. prefers his stay to going away. I ask, is not this stay voluntary? I think nobody will doubt it: and yet, being locked fast in, it is evident he is not at liberty not to stay, he has not freedom to be gone. So that liberty is not an idea belonging to volition, or preferring; but to the person having the power of doing, or forbearing to do, according as the mind shall choose or direct. Our idea of liberty reaches as far as that power, and no farther. For whatever restraint comes to check that power, or compulsion takes away that indifferency of ability to act, or to forbear acting, there liberty, and our notion of it, presently ceases ..."

–John Locke, Essay Concerning Human Understanding

Campus Rumpus I–IV

"In their temper of mind they were socially minded citizens, by no means self-assertive, not unduly anxious for power, and in favour of a tolerant world where, within the limits of the criminal law, every man was free to do as he pleased. They were good natured men of the world, urbane and kindly ..."

–Bertrand Russell, The History of Western Philosophy

The Master's Delight

"Imagine a club the new members of which are always shanghaied. When a new member is wanted, a press-gang is sent to find a suitable candidate. When one is found, he is dragged to the club's premises and forcibly inducted. The induction ceremony (we may imagine) is so impressive that members are fiercely loyal to the club as long as they remain members. But few if any members remain members long. When a member is exhausted by his efforts on the club's behalf, and after his resources have been appropriated and placed in the club's treasury, he is ruthlessly expelled. The membership of the club is therefore in constant flux. The one stable thing about the club is its constitution (which, of course, is not an identifiable object but rather a complex set of dispositions and intentions that is maintained by the assiduous indoctrination of new members). One important feature of this constitution is its prescription that whenever anyone ceases to be a member, a press-gang is to be sent out to capture a replacement for him, someone who is as much like the way he was when he was inducted as is possible. As a consequence, the club 'looks' much the same from one year to the next, despite the continual replacement of its members . . ."

–Peter van Inwagen, *Material Beings*

Cloakroom, 1984

"His opinions are harmonious, and he desires the same things with all his soul; and therefore he wishes for himself what is good and what seems so, and does it (for it is characteristic of the good man to work out the good), and does so for his own sake (for he does it for the sake of the intellectual element in him, which is thought to be the man himself); and he wishes himself to live and be preserved, and especially the element by virtue of which he thinks. For existence is good to the virtuous man, and each man wishes himself what is good. . .; he wishes for this only on condition of being whatever he is; and the element that thinks would seem to be the individual man, or to be so more than any other element in him. And such a man wishes to live with himself; for he does so with pleasure, since the memories of his past acts are delightful and his hopes for the future are good, and therefore pleasant. His mind is well stored too with subjects of contemplation. And he grieves and rejoices, more than any other, with himself; for the same thing I always painful, and the same thing always pleasant, and not one thing at one time and another at another; *he has just about nothing to regret.*"

–Aristotle, *Nichomachean Ethics*

Empty Man IV: Abbie (2018)

"[i]n their official sittings [the philosophers] discussed highly abstract matters, but in their spare time they would touch on all the most thorny questions of European politics. I observed, with astonished admiration, that national bias hardly ever showed itself in these discussions. The severe logical training to which these men submitted themselves had, it appeared, rendered them immune to the infection of passionate dogma."

–Bertrand Russell, *Polemic*

Mycorrhizae

"Suppose that medical science has developed a technique whereby a surgeon can completely remove a person's brain from his head, examine or operate on it, and then put it back in his skull (regrafting the nerves, blood-vessels, and so forth) without causing death or permanent injury... One day a surgeon discovers that an assistant has made a horrible mistake. Two men, a Mr Brown and a Mr Robinson, had been operated on for brain tumours, and brain extractions had been performed on both of them. At the end of the operations, however, the assistant inadvertently put Brown's brain in Robinson's head, and Robinson's brain in Brown's head. One of these men immediately dies, but the other , the one with Robinson's body and Brown's brain, eventually regains consciousness. Let us call the latter 'Brownson'... He recognises Brown's wife and family (whom Robinson had never met), and is able to describe in detail events in Brown's life, always describing them as events in his own life. Of Robinson's past life he evidences no knowledge at all. Over a period of time he is observed to display all of the personality traits, mannerisms, interests, likes and dislikes, and so on that had previously characterized Brown, and to act and talk in ways completely alien to the old Robinson ..."

–Sydney Shoemaker, *Self-Knowledge and Self-Identity*

A Manifesto for Horror As Critique of Analytic Philosophy

"To build up systems of the world, like Heine's German professor who knit together fragments of life and made an intelligible system out of them, is not, I believe, any more feasible than the discovery of the philosopher's stone. What is feasible is the understanding of general forms, and the division of traditional problems into a number of separate and less baffling questions. "Divide and conquer" is the maxim of success here as elsewhere ..."

–Bertrand Russell, *Mysticism and Logic and Other Essays*

Select Bibliography

Ahmed, Sara, *Living a Feminist Life*, Duke University Press (2017)

Ahmed, Sara, *feministkilljoys.com* (2013–)

Andrews, Kehinde, "How to stay radical within an institution", TEDx talk (2017) https://www.youtube.com/watch?v=VFUymWxfrkQ

Applebaum, Barbara, *Being White, Being Good: White Complicity, White Moral Responsibility and Social Justice*, Lexington Books (2010)

Bain, Zara, "Is there such a thing as 'white ignorance' in British Education?", *Ethics and Education*, special issue edited by Judith Suissa and Darren Chetty 13:1, 4–21 (2018)

Baraitser, Lisa, *Enduring Time*, Bloomsbury (2017)

Beebee, Helen and Saul, Jenny, "SWIP Report on Women in Philosophy in the UK", www.swipuk.org (2009)

Benhabib, Seyla, "Feminism and postmodernism: An uneasy alliance", *Filosoficky Casopis* 46:5, 803–818 (1998)

Bentley, Abigail and Chetty, Darren, "DwellingTogether" (2018) https://dwellingtogetherfilm.wordpress.com/2018/03/19/the-journey-begins/

Borden, Lizzie (dir.) *Born in Flames*, USA (1983)

Bourdieu, Pierre, *Homo Academicus*, trans. Peter Collier, Stanford University Press (1988)

Bourdieu, Pierre, *Masculine Domination*, trans. Richard Nice, Stanford University Press (2002)

Bouteldja, Houria, *Whites, Jews, and Us: Towards a Politics of Revolutionary Love*, MIT Press (2016)

Butcher, Daisy (ed.) *Evil Roots: Killer Tales of the Botanical Gothic*, British Library Tales of the Weird (2020)

Butler, Judith, *Gender Trouble: Feminism and the Subversion of Identity*, Routledge (1990)

Carter, Angela, *The Bloody Chamber and Other Stories*, Gollancz (1979)

Chetty, Darren, "Racism as 'Reasonableness': Philosophy for Children and the Gated Community of Inquiry", *Ethics and Education*, special issue edited by Judith Suissa and Darren Chetty, 13:1, 1–4 (2018)

~~Coleman~~, Nathaniel Adam Tobias, *The Duty to Miscegenate*, doctoral thesis, (2013)

~~Coleman~~, Nathaniel Adam Tobias, "Why isn't my professor black?", http://www.dtmh.ucl.ac.uk/videos/isnt-professor-black-nathaniel-coleman/

Dostoevsky, Fyodor, *Notes from Underground* (1864)

Dotson, Kristie, "Conceptualising Epistemic Oppression", *Social Epistemology*, 28:2, 115–138 (2014)

Doston, Kristie, "How is this Paper Philosophy?", *Comparative Philosophy*, 3:1, 3–29 (2013)

Fisher, Mark, *The Weird and the Eerie*, Repeater Books (2016)

Fricker, Miranda, *Epistemic Injustice: Power and the Ethics of Knowing*, Oxford University Press (2007)

Gilman, Charlotte Perkins, "When I was a witch" *Forerunner* (1910)

Haber, Mark (interview with David Naimon), *Between the Covers* (2019) https://tinhouse.com/podcast/mark-haber-reinhardts-garden/

Haslanger, Sally, *Resisting Reality: Social Construction and Social Critique*, Oxford University Press (2013)

Hill Collins, Patricia, *Black Feminist Thought: Knowledge, Consciousness, and the Politics of Empowerment*, Hyman (1990)

hooks, bell, *Teaching to Transgress: Education as the Practice of Freedom*, Routledge (1994)

Jackson, Shirley, *The Lottery and Other Stories*, Farrar, Straus (1949)

Jackson, Shirley, *The Haunting of Hill House*, Viking Press (1959)

Jackson, Shirley, *We Have Always Lived in the Castle*, Viking Press (1962)

Jackson, Shirley, "Afternoon in Linen", in *The Lottery and Other Stories*, Farrar, Staus (1949)

James, M.R., *Collected Ghost Stories*, Edward Arnold (1931)

Jemisin, N.K. *How Long 'til Black Future Month*, Orbit (2018)

Jemisin, N.K. (interview with David Naimon), *Between the Covers* (2020) https://tinhouse.com/podcast/n-k-jemisin-the-city-we-became/

Kristeva, Julia, *Powers of Horror: An Essay on Abjection*, Columbia University Press (1982)

Le Doeuff, Michèle, *The Philosophical Imaginary*, trans. Colin Gordon, Stanford University Press (1990)

Ligotti, Thomas, *Songs of a Dead Dreamer*, Silver Scarab Press (1989)

Lispector, Clarice, *The Passion According to G.H.*, Penguin Modern Classics (1964)

Lovibond, Sabina, *Essays on Ethics and Feminism*, Oxford University Press (2015)

Manne, Kate, *Down Girl: The Logic of Misogyny*, Oxford University Press (2017)

Melville, Herman, "Bartleby, the Scrivener: A Story of Wall Street", *Putnam's Magazine* (1853)

Mills, Charles, *The Racial Contract*, Cornell University Press (1997)

Morrison, Toni, *Beloved*, Alfred A. Knopf Inc. (1987)

Morrison, Toni, *Playing in the Dark: Whiteness and the Literary Imagination*, Harvard University Press (1992)

Narayan, Uma, "Working Together across Difference: Some Considerations on Emotions and Political Practice", *Hypatia* 3:2, 31–47 (1988)

Peele, Jordon (dir.) *Get Out*, Universal Pictures (2017)

Roupenian, Kristen and Deborah Treisman (in conversation), "'Afternoon in Linen' by Shirley Jackson", *The New Yorker Fiction* podcast (2020) https://www.newyorker.com/podcast/fiction/kristen-roupenian-reads-shirley-jackson

Sartre, Jean-Paul, *Nausea* (1938)

Trigg, Dylan, *Topophobia: A Phenomenology of Anxiety*, Bloomsbury (2016)

Warren, Calvin L., *Ontological Terror: Blackness, Nihilism, and Emancipation*, Duke University Press (2018)

Acknowledgements

My thanks to Liza Thompson, without whom this book would have been both practically and emotionally impossible. Thanks too to Lucy Russell, Jodie Rose and the team at Bloomsbury for conducting the process so capably.

It is said that the Cambridge writer and academic, M.R. James read his ghost stories, fire-side, to colleagues at Christmas. In this spirit, early drafts of these texts were shared over Friday night dinners with friends, including Kim Bonnar, Laurencia Saenz Benavides, Niki Fitzgerald, Diarmaid Keliher, Esther McManus, Jonathan Nassim and Lou Tyson, who were all generous enough to indulge me in my reading.

Jonathan Nassim has been the staunchest of companions in my explorations of the miseries of academia. During the first COVID Lockdown in the UK, he was the recipient of weekly recordings of these texts and offered valuable insight and support. If they were written to comfort anyone other than myself, it was for him.

Other fellow travellers through the backwaters of UK academia include: Veromi Arsiradam, Zara Bain, Dara Bascara, Helen Beebee, Joanna Burch-Brown, Darren Chetty, Nathaniel Adam Tobias ~~Coleman~~, Elianna Fetterolf, James Fisher, Anil Gomes, Joshua Habgoode-Coote, Elizabeth Hannon, Cadence Kinsey, Nadia Mehdi, Chris Meyns, Clare Moriarty, Deborah Mühlebach, Judith Suissa,

William Tattersdill and Duncan Taylor. I was never happy in academia, but I have often been happy in their company. Helen and Judith deserve special mention for providing much-needed support in undiscussable institutional settings. I am also particularly grateful to Veromi, Zara, Darren, Nadia and Chris for joining me on co-authorship projects – and for tipping my work/life balance much more enjoyably towards the latter (as well as Andrew, Rageshri and Christie).

In 2016, I was fortunate enough to travel to Japan where I interviewed Hidé Ishiguro. Meeting her and engaging with her history in London philosophy was a highlight of my brief career in academia and an inspiration, sadly, for some of the thoughts found in these pages.

Over the last few years, I have relied heavily on the support of my friends. Thanks to Vivienne Watson, Florence Bullough and Luke Massey, companions on journeys into space (Star Trek) and deeper underground (Dungeons and Dragons). Thanks to Nenna Orie Chuku, for her acerbic comments about my cooking, to Alice Franklin for her irregular voice-notes, and to everyone at the Platform Youth Hub, especially Anna Bennett, Lottie Manzie, Semothy Jones and Juma Woodhouse. Thanks to Mike Smith, for wearing shorts all year round, and to Emily Berry, who attends to the swelter of worldly anxieties while helping others (me) to face them. Thanks also to Ruth and Pete. Thank you to the irrepressible Daniel Pollendine. Thank you to R.T. for taking me seriously (and persuading me to do the same). Thanks to Maeve Duval, Maya Kalaya, Genny Hawkens, Margaret Jacobi, Will Jessop and Sophie Waterhouse.

Writing is hard at the best of times – and enforced isolation during a pandemic is far from the best of times. I have felt more connected to other writers through listening to David Naimon on *Between the Covers* as well as Deborah Treisman of the *New Yorker Fiction Podcast* and the *Birmingham Literary Festival Podcast*, produced by the inimitable Shantel Edwards. Few people have helped me understand the wonder of the written word quite as much as Shantel. I write because I find it exhausting to talk, and alongside Emily and Vivienne, Shantel is one of my most gentle and generous readers. I have also been fortunate enough to have this manuscript read by the caring and careful Andy West. Eva Ibbotson was among my very first readers and for that I am extremely grateful.

With respect to our non-human friends, I extend my thanks to: Archie, Bambam, Luna, Marlowe, Podger, Puggles, Socks, Suzie, Xena and Willow.

It is impossible to compass here all the debts I owe to Esther McManus, with whom I have shared my horrors too freely. I am grateful to her for her encouragement, kindness and support, her insight and her wit, and many other things besides.

Thanks are due, too, to my birth family as well as my chosen one (the latter, in fact, contains the former): to the extended Ferners and Mosses, to my parents, for being unflappably supportive, financially and morally (as well as unflappable); to my brother, Dave (and Medi) and my sister, Harriet (and James). At the time of writing, I am also thirteen-months an uncle – and my last vote of thanks is to my niece, Talia Jean, who provides convincing evidence that, in some cases at least, existence is a form of perfection.

Declaration of earnings

I was paid no advance for this book and will receive 20% royalties.

Credits

Editorial

Editorial Director: Emily Drewe
Publisher: Liza Thompson
Assistant Editor: Lucy Russell

Marketing

Marketing Manager: Brenna Armstrong
Senior Marketing Manager: Joseph Kreuser

Production

Senior Production Editor: Giles Herman
Project Management: Merv Honeywood

Operations

Academic Inventory Manager: Sue Behrent
Inventory Planner: Cathy von Ameln

Sales

Associate Director of Sales: Mathew Nichols
UK Academic and Professional Sales Director: Matthew Emery
Sales Manager: Sarah Ailsby

Design

Designer: Ben Anslow
Artworker: Jess Stevens

Contracts

Head of Contracts: Christelle Chamouton
Contracts Assistant: Almudena Gutierrez

Rights

Head of Academic Rights: Joanna Sharland
Senior Rights Manager: Jenny Redhead
Rights Manager: Alison Faulkner
Rights Manager: Isabel Lopez Ruiz
Rights Manager: Sinead Tully

Finance

Group Finance Director: Penny Scott-Bayfield
Group Financial Controller: Tim Mehta
Head of Royalties: Paul Tokely
Head of Group Finance: Scott Rigg

Legal

Group General Counsel and Company Secretary: Maya Abu-Deeb
Legal Counsel: Keith Rooney

Author

A.M. Moskovitz and S.K. Lang are pseudonyms of Adam Ferner, a freelance writer and researcher living and working in London. Adam completed his PhD in analytic metaphysics before going on to author and co-author several books including *Think Differently* (2016), *Philosophy* (with Zara Bain and Nadia Mehdi, 2018), *How to Disagree* (with Darren Chetty, 2018) and *The Philosophers' Library* (with Chris Meyns, 2021).